THE DAY
PICASSO
DIED

ISBN # 978-0-557-52988-9

PART ONE

The guy looked cop.

The guy dressed cop (Who'd be wearing a suit, shirt with button-down collar and tie, plus a pair of wrap-around shades at <u>midnight</u> for Christ sakes?).

Hell, the guy even *smelled* cop.

How's a cop smell? Like aftershave laid on too thick to mask jailhouse stench. Like nicotine under the fingernails. Like stale coffee and donuts at 3 A. M.

That's how the cops who periodically haul my ass down to the tank after I've had one too many shots and beers smell. Not that they're a nasty lot, mind you; there's the occasional bad egg, but most are pretty understanding. At least the ones who know *me* are.

But this cop *didn't* know me. He was an out-of-towner for sure. He flagged my cab down, standing on a street corner where *nobody* in a suit has been seen since after World War Two, and most people lock their doors and draw their shades after dark, hypnotized by the boob tube and noshing Twinkies. Me, I don't own a TV (Or a car for that matter. I drink, and drinking and driving don't mix. Besides, I get more than enough time behind the wheel, driving twelve hour shifts from 6 P. M. to 6 A. M., weekdays.) I paint and drink on weekends. Oil paintings, not houses. Shots of whiskey and beer chasers, not water.

I knew why he was in town. There'd been a lot of cops in plainclothes doing undercover work lately, due to the massive influx of whores that had inundated the city like roaches in a cold-water flat. And with the whores had come drugs, murders, beatings. City Council had had a fire lit under their rumps by irate, do-gooder citizens and the P. D. had responded, arresting and transporting two dozen ladies of the evening to the Illinois line, effectively shagging their asses back to Chicago, from whence they had surely come. The cops had alerted news photographers, of course, and the ensuing pictures had mollified the Sunday school crowd.

But only for a while. The problem was still there. Whores were knocking on windows of family station wagons; Dad driving, Mom snuggled next to him, kiddies in the back seat; inquiring if the man of the house wanted to part with five bucks for an immoral sex act. The sordid tales had hit the *Chicago Tribune*; not exactly the best p. r. for a factory town down on its luck. There was also the issue of pimps transporting minors across state lines for the sole purpose of prostitution, which was a federal offense.

Which meant F.B.I., and which meant you had guys in business suits at 11:30 P. M. on a Sunday night in a rough-and-tumble neighborhood, flagging down a cabby with the sole intent of trying to coerce said cabby into setting up a liaison with a lady of the evening so you could bust said cabby and lady.

No way, Jose, I mumbled as I pulled over to pick up Mr. F.B.I. I knew his game, so he wasn't going to bust me. Besides, it was a slow night and I needed the fare. I figured I'd fix his ass but good and get paid for it, to boot.

"Thanks, pal," he said as he slid into the back seat. (See? Who else would call you 'pal' but a cop?)

"Where to, mack?" I asked. I was on my best stereotypical behavior that night. I'd act the part of the atypical cabby. Wisecracking salt-of-the-earth sage.

He leaned over with his elbows on the back of my seat, his stale-coffee-and-donut breath hot on the back of my neck. "How about showing me where the girls are, pal?" he asked.

"Girls?" I was playing stupid. I could show him where the girls were, of course. Local girls who weren't for sale but would like a snappily-dressed dude like him and take him around the world for the price of a few drinks and a good meal.

"You know what I mean," he said, winking. I knew he was winking because he'd removed the shades and I'd tilted my rear view and was watching him closely.

I winked back, broadly (Big kidder, me) and said, "I don't know what you mean." Then I held a finger in the air like I was struck by the light.

"Oh, *girls*, you mean?" I said. I swear he jumped six inches in his seat. Thought he had me nailed for sure.

"Yeah. Where can I find one? For the night?"

Like I was thinking he wasn't looking to get laid? Or pretending to?

"Night's almost over, pal," I replied. "But I know where there's girls."

He squirmed in his seat, impatient to make the bust and put another decent, hard-working joe in jail. "Okay," he said. "Let's go."

I drove him through the central city. We're only 100,000 souls in this factory town, but we've got a few neighborhoods that I'd put up against the worst Chicago has to offer and I took him to one of those, pulling up to the curb at Sonny's Cafe, which isn't a cafe but a hangout for transvestites of the colored persuasion. In fact, Sonny himself, outfitted in a sequined nightgown and fishnet stockings that can't mask his chiseled calves (Sonny plays right tackle for the Gladiators, a local semi-pro football team) was parked outside the front door under his neon Budweiser sign, puffing on one of those skinny mega-length ladies' cigarettes, holding a tete a tete with whitebread Petey

Wilson, who rumor has it was going to have one of those sex change operations that seemed to be all the rage these days.

Sonny sees me and his face lights up like his Bud sign. He saunters over to the cab and leans through my open front window. "Johnn-eee Jump," he says. "What's cookin', sugar?"

I jerk a thumb in the direction of Mr. Incognito in the back seat, who is now plastered up against the upholstery like a cat to a tree trunk when he spies Sonny's six foot two, two hundred forty-five pounds of rock'm, sock'm iron-hard muscle which even the spangled nightgown cannot hide.

"Guy says he's looking for 'girls,' Sonny," I said, winking broadly and letting the wink reflect in the rear view so Mr. F.B.I. can see.

"My, my, my, my," said Sonny, opening the back door and reaching in and pulling out Suit and Shades, who tries to resist but Sonny is just too much for him. "How they hangin', sweet cakes?"

The guy started fumbling for his badge, mumbling something about F.B.I. (See, can I peg 'em, or what?), but Sonny got a half nelson on his scrawny neck so the words came out something like a terrified squeak. With the suit wrapped under one arm, Sonny leans through the cab's window again. He placed a gentle hand on my shoulder.

"I owe you one, Sonny," I said, gently peeling his ebony meat hooks off my flannel shirt.

"Someday, sugar," he replied. "I'm gonna collect."

"Not my cup of tea, Sonny. You know that."

"Uh huh," he said unconvincingly. Then he straightened up, J. Edgar Hoover still locked in the half nelson, squirming. "I know what we'll do with this guy. Spankin' Frank's inside. Ought to cure him of tryin' to hustle the city's finest cab driver."

Suit and Shades managed one sentence before Sonny dragged him inside the bar. "I'll get you," he hissed.

"No you won't," I replied and drove away. I was six blocks gone before I realized I hadn't collected my fare.

***

I pulled down my visor and stared at the picture-postcard I had secured there with a bobby pin plucked from Sweet Lorraine's head. Sweet Lorraine is seventy years old, horny as hell and every cabby who gets her call has to suffer the same routine, fighting off the old lady's pawing mitts while trying to collect their fare. One of Lorraine's swirling white hairs was still lodged in the bobby pin and snaked across the picture.

It's one of my man Pablo's best. "Les Demoiselles d'Avignon." Picasso called it his "first exorcism-painting," which it surely is. Man, to be that self-assured with the brush! To put down the strokes and create an entirely new art form, all the while spitting in the face of conventionalism!

That's what makes Pablo the greatest, no matter if he says thing like, "If I spit they'll frame the spit and call it great art." That's what he often did; spit at them, and they <u>did</u> call it great art. But it's the man's towering achievement. He not only has the ability to create monumental art, he also cons the pretenders who think themselves aficionados: the white wine and brie cheese crowd that wouldn't know great art from their own pathetic, puckered assholes.

I purchased the postcard at Chicago's Art Institute, where I enjoy spending many solitary afternoons, wandering the marbled halls, challenged by great art. The one thing that matters in this world.

Which is why I am a cabby. It allows me the time to paint and to perform that most important of artistic tasks: to observe. Hey, how can you paint if you first don't learn how to *see*? And then to comprehend?

It didn't take much effort or artistic experience to see her, however. Mini-skirt hugging a tight round bottom. Long legs, high breasts. Auburn locks chopped in a nineteen-twenties-style Flapper bob with Prince Valiant bangs. A real piece of work. You could see it in the way she moved; confident, without the obvious "Look at me," come on you see in so many beautiful women.

She strolled coolly past the other three cabs, each cabby standing with door open, motioning her inside as they attempted to hustle the fare. Old toothless Freddie drooled as she walked by, rubbing his crotch with one hand, holding his cab door with the other, hopping from one foot to the other like he was tap dancing on hot coals. As if she was going to ever hop into his cab!

I had just pulled into the lot at the Chicago and Northwestern station, hoping to snag a fare off the midnight train. Pickings had been slim of late, ever since City Council had closed most of the strip bars, but an occasional straggler still got off the train now and again and could end up being a live one.

She opened the door to my hack and slid inside. A rich, buttery scent of lilacs and roses trailed her into the cab and curled serpentine-like between the front seat and the dash.

"Where to, lady?" I asked. I get real eloquent around beautiful women, as you can see.

She pointed to my visor, which was still down, and said: "Les Demoiselles d'Avignon. A great painting, don't you think?"

Right then and there she had my heart strings.

I replied in the affirmative. "Not only a great painting, lady. A great statement. My man Pablo."

She scrunched her nose, as if in deep thought. "I disagree. The man can paint. But he's a huckster when it comes to the statement thing."

Man! I was ready to grab her beautiful shoulders and shake some sense into her. Pablo Picasso? A huckster? But I held my cool. She was beautiful and it seemed she knew her art, but she was a fare and the night was skinny in the cash department. So I repeated, "Where to, lady?"

"I came here to disappear," she replies. "Take me somewhere where we can have a quiet drink, and discuss Mr. Picasso. I'll pay you for your time. I just need some company."

Hell, I didn't NEED any more direction than that.

***

Pablo was born at eleven-fifteen p.m., October twenty-five, eighteen-eighty-one, not breathing. They gave up the baby as stillborn, with the exception of one of Pablo's uncles, who was a skilled doctor. Doc Uncle took a deep drag off his cigar and blew a puff of smoke up the baby's nose. That jarred baby Pablo awake, all right.

That was the first and last time anyone blew smoke up Picasso's nose. But not, of course, the other way around. Old Pablo has spent his life blowing smoke up the nose of the establishment. And as I sat watching the fare I had recently scored (she stirring a finger in her glass, tinkling the ice cubes like tiny bells), I wondered if she was blowing smoke up the nose of your favorite cabby.

Her name was Suzy Anger, and she had come up from Chi-town for the weekend for "a little r & r," as she put it.

"R & r" stood for stiff drinks; whiskey on the rocks, smoky fire as it slid down the throat, beer chaser. A potent combo, and one that was working its way into the whiskey-sodden brain of yours truly as I matched her glass for glass. Hell, she was paying for my time and buying the drinks; who was I to refuse?

We sucked 'em down and talked art. From Leonardo to DeKooning we discussed brush strokes, color, perspective and vision. She expressed admiration for the Siennese religious mystics of thirteenth century Italy, who pre-dated the Renaissance by two hundred years and were basically wiped out by the Black Death that swept across Europe like one of the plagues Yahweh visited on the Egyptians.

"Why does a talented man like you drive a taxi?" she asked. She had unbuttoned the top two buttons of her silk blouse, revealing a pronounced cleavage like the chiseled shadows in a canvas by Caravaggio. My eyes had rested there, and she seemed to welcome them.

"How do you know I'm talented?" I asked her breasts.

"You smell like turp (slang for turpentine for you Philistines); you have paint under your fingernails and most important, you have the fire of a true artist in your eyes."

"Oh, you see all that in me?"

"I do."

Mad Dan, proprietor of the corner saloon, sauntered to our booth. "'Scuse me. Need another round, Johnny?"

There were four miracles here. First, Mad Dan doesn't wait tables. Anyone who wants a drink in his joint has to belly up to the bar. Second, he was wearing a clean apron. Third, his hair was neatly parted and combed down with a gob of Brylcreem (sort of like Alfalfa in the "Little Rascals," sans cowlick). Fourth, he said 'excuse me.' an unheard-of phenomenon. I ascribed all these miracles to the presence of my beautiful fare. In fact, if Mad Dan's tongue hung any lower he could have licked that beautiful cleavage without bending his neck. He wasn't alone. As usual, the bar was entirely stag and every eye was fixed on the haunting Suzy Anger.

Here she was, buying _me_ drinks and paying for _my_ time. Eat your hearts out, fellas.

Some of them were doing more than eating out their hearts, however. There were a few died-in-the-wool rednecks from Mississippi and Alabama way; factory workers with those banjo-picker hardscrabble blue eyes and flat, meaty faces who took umbrage that I would be imbibing with a beautiful white woman, entertaining the thought of a roll in the hay. Their eyes burned holes into the back of my neck, and I thought I could hear hammers cocking on upraised forty-fives.

The tension could be because my long hair sprouted from under a red bandanna, and I sport a golden hoop earring.

Oh, I am also black.

Not black, actually. Quadroon is the polite term, I believe. My hair is slightly kinky and I have a hint of coffee-color to my complexion. My nose flares slightly and my lips are a bit thick (Ladies have called my mouth 'sensual.' I forgive them the grammatical error). My mother was part Dutch, my father, Polish. But my mother's mother was a beautiful blue-black lady from Louisiana; a woman who'd spent her entire life raising babies and picking cotton. She was the most caring, understanding person I have ever known and was the one human being who encouraged me in my art. My father drank his short life away, passing on at the age of forty; and shortly afterward my mother took off for parts unknown. I was nine years old.

Which left the raising of yours truly to Grandma Jones, who left her ancestral shack in the Louisiana delta and took the Greyhound bus to Chicago and then farther north to the grimy factory city my parents called home. She took in washing and raised me with a willow switch, wholesome food and plenty of love and encouragement.

She also told me never to compromise, to make my life my own and once I made a decision, to never look back. And believe it or not that old black lady, hard from the years on the delta, face wrinkled like a lump of tar gone soft in the heat, turned me on to fine art and to Pablo.

"I don't know what it is, honey," she'd say to me when we thumbed through the big picture books of art I brought home from the school library. She turned the books sideways, studying Picasso's crazy paintings with a quizzical eye. "But I 'tink d' man has got *somet'in'*, me."

I changed my name when Grandma Jones died, and disavowed my parents. My given name was Johnathon Gumpowski. I cut out the 'owski,' but the name didn't ring true. Whoever heard of somebody named 'Gump?' So I changed 'Gump' to 'Jump,' and Johnathon to Johnny.

Johnny Jump, that's me. The quarter-black (Sounds like quarter-horse, doesn't it? A stallion with noble blood lines) sitting with the beautiful white woman in the redneck bar. To the callous southern faces staring at me, any black man who even entertained the thought of sex with a white woman would be guilty of rape. Arrested and promptly busted out of jail, dragged to the nearest tree limb and lynched. If these men had heard of the civil rights movement, Martin Luther King and the end of Jim Crow, you couldn't tell it by the cold hate that reflected off their faces. I was thinking that it was maybe time to move to a more liberal climate; one of the long-hair saloons where we would be lost in the crowd.

"You didn't answer my question," said Suzy Anger.

I was engaged in a staring contest with a redneck in bib overalls and a John Deere baseball cap. His beer gut and flabby arms told me I could take him in a second. I am, after all, six feet tall and two hundred solid pounds. I keep a pair of fifty pound dumbbells in my apartment and work out regularly with them: presses, curls, one-armed-rows, that sort of thing. To put it bluntly, I'm a hell of a lot stronger than your average cabby, and yon redneck caused me no real alarm. It was his ten other friends that worried me.

I slowly took my eyes off him and looked at Suzy Anger. "Why an 'arteest' like me is driving a cab?"

"Yes."

"Because, as Willie Sutton said, 'that's where the money is.'"

"Willie Sutton robbed banks."

"I would, too, if I could get away with it."

"Willie Sutton didn't. Get away with it, I mean."

I coughed into my hand, clearing my throat. "Look, lady. It's difficult believing someone as beautiful as you . . ."

"Thank you," she interrupted, reaching out and lightly touching my hands. An audible groan emanated from the redneck section of the bar. I pulled my hand away. No use tempting fate. Or a world-class ass-whipping.

"You're welcome. Why would someone as beautiful as you bother herself with somebody like me?"

"You don't think you're attractive?"

"Sure, to the girls I know. But they come from different social strata. You reek of money, and status. In fact, you shouldn't be grabbing cabs in this town. You should have a chauffeured limo waiting curbside, complete with TV and wet bar."

"You think I'm wealthy?"

"I do. So what is your pleasure? You want something, I know that. I can see it in your eyes. You're squirming in your seat like you've got a big itch."

She looked me square in the face and smiled, flashing perfect Colgate commercial teeth. "You're sassy, aren't you? How'd you like to come work for me? You could limo me around Chicago, and paint on your free time."

"Uh uh. I answer to nobody and I like it that way. I have a feeling that if I come to work for you, there'd be a golden chain fastened right into my nose."

She laughed "Ha!" in answer.

I was going to make that suggestion to move on to another location, but she motioned to Mad Dan for another round and he hustled over with two more whiskies with beer chasers.

"On the house," he said, setting them gently on the table.

I stared at him in open-mouthed astonishment.

"Can't a guy buy a drink once in a while?" he asked sheepishly.

Miracle number five.

"All right," she said, sipping at her drink. "I'll tell you what my pleasure is." It was her fourth boilermaker and she was displaying zero effects. I had seen plenty of big girls down more alcohol and take it in stride, but for a woman of her modest dimensions it was an impressive feat.

"I was looking for you specifically. I was told you might be at the station, hustling the train," she said.

I smiled and nodded, remembering Mark Twain's maxim about it being better to keep your mouth shut and appear stupid rather than opening it and removing all doubt.

She set a photograph on the table between us. "You know him?"

He was maybe twenty years younger in the photo and there was a spark of youthful hope in his wide eyes; but there was no mistaking who it was. The flabby jowls were there, but abbreviated. And the round head and wide eyes. The protruding lower lip, soft chin that seemed to melt into his neck.

"Sure," I replied. "That's old Virgil. He bunks at my place. He's got no place else to go."

"So I heard," she said, thoughtfully fingering the photograph.

"What do you want with him? I'm all he's got. He's a lost soul; a man without a family."

"Maybe to you he is. But he's my uncle, and with my grandfather's recent death, he's inherited a lot of money."

"Oh yeah? How much?"

"One million dollars."

Okay, so maybe that groan she heard was my astonishment as my jaw dropped and my mouth opened, yawning like a cavern.

One *MILLION* dollars?

"No shit?" I said, rhapsodizing on the pure poetry of the moment.

"Precisely."

Hell, with that kind of money you could *buy* "Le Demoiselles d'Avignon."

***

I maintain a cozy one bedroom apartment above a local insurance agency located on the downtown strip. The area has gone to hell, with most of the old-line retailers moving to new strip malls on the city's periphery. The banks are still there, and plenty of taverns but a quarter of the storefronts are vacant, windows soaped to prevent any of the curious from staring through them to steal a free glimpse of the emptiness inside. Hell, people; this is America. You don't give anything away. If the government could find a way to tax the air we breathe, I'm sure they'd do it.

I approached the downtown retail association (what was left of it) and offered to paint the blank windows in a mural-type theme: a biblical drama featuring the parting of the Red Sea by Richard Nixon with a surrounding cast comprised of Mark Spitz, Archie Bunker and scenes from the war in Viet Nam, but of course was turned down. What I should have done was proposed a Ronald McDonald epic: the fuzzy feel-good clown stuffing tasteless burgers down the throats of American children, fattening them up for the eventual heart attack. Chubby cheeks like primary color balloons. And punctuated the mural with plenty of those obnoxious, ubiquitous yellow smile faces.

That would have turned *them* on, I bet.

Ned, my landlord and proprietor of the struggling insurance agency located directly below my apartment, accepts a painting a month in lieu of rent. He is a hook-nosed man with thick glasses, a pathetic squeak of a voice and a dumpy, pear-shaped body. He prefers paintings of nudes in the realistic style so each month I take the time to coerce Jennifer, a female acquaintance and sometime girlfriend to pose in the nude for me. I change the poses of course, to give the paintings variety; as well as the size and shape of her breasts and the color of her hair. (I once gave her lush blonde pubic hair done up in a natural wave like a Breck girl, and Ned nearly went off the deep end). Ned believes he is receiving a rendering of a different woman every month, but it is always Jennifer. I figure I am not cheating him, as he is playing out his fantasies with the canvases. Under the influence, I painted a naked Jennifer riding a plummeting A-bomb like a bronco, breasts bouncing, waving a black-banded cowboy hat ala Slim Pickens in "Dr. Strangelove," but Ned would have none of it. I sold it to a traveling salesman I met in a bar for twenty-five dollars and a pitcher of beer. (I don't come cheap, as you can see).

As I parked the cab in my alleyway parking spot, I wondered if the seductive Suzy Anger would allow me to paint her in the nude. I would have loved to. She must have read my lecherous thoughts.

"Taking me up to see your etchings?" she quipped as I held the door open for her.

"Wasn't that a bad line from a bad movie?" I couldn't help watching her long legs as the mini-skirt rode high on her thighs as she stepped from the cab.

"Probably," she replied, looking around the dark alley. "You live here? This looks like a great spot for a gangland hit"

I had thought that same thought more than once, many times peeking behind (and inside) the dented garbage cans to see if someone had deposited a corpse there. A man perhaps of swarthy, Italian visage; one bullet hole neatly punctuating the spot where the bridge of his nose bifurcated his eyes. To my chagrin, the alley, though it was the perfect setting, remained free of corpses.

"Upstairs," I said, gesturing to the two flights of wooden steps leading to the tiny wood-framed porch that constituted my patio. It's where I sometimes barbecued thick steaks on a hibachi while old Virgil regaled me with tales of the south seas; sarong-clad, nut-brown females and white sand beaches. Not that he's ever been there. I believe that Virgil plays Gauguin of the imagination, creating pretty pictures on the canvas of his mind. Some people would call it bullshit. I prefer to interpret it as a sort of rococo poetry. Creativity on a spectral plane.

Old Virgil is also the purveyor of the world's greatest pick-up lines. He once wrapped an arm around Sweet Lorraine and nibbled her ear. "Come with me to Florida, my little angel," he intoned in that nasal, W. C. Fields voice of his.

"And we'll pick oranges in the golden sun, diadems from the beaches."

Pure poetry, and it elicited a like response.

Lorraine placed a lip-lock on him that actually popped his false teeth out of his mouth when she disengaged. She consequently became the one female he assiduously avoids.

When I first saw him he was fast asleep with his head in the urinal at the Kitty Kat Lounge (The Kitty Kat is the black velvet painting capitol of the Midwest. The walls are festooned with schlock tigers, wide-eyed kids in the post-Keane style and Elvis in spangled jumpsuits), alone and unwanted. I took him home, semi-sobered him up and decided to allow him to sleep a few nights on my living room sofa, as he was broke and without a place to stay. The few nights had become two years, and I didn't mind. He didn't eat much, kept the apartment clean and mostly sponged his beer money off other indigents.

He didn't snore and kept out of my way when Jennifer visited for her monthly posing sessions. He was damned good company, too. I had rendered more than one of his fantasies onto canvas: starry nights, sailing ships, beautiful women, gods and goddesses, flasks of wine. A Falstaffian bacchanalia of the mind that I laid down in thick layers of primary colors in broad, aggressive brush strokes.

And here was this stunning female telling me the man I had rescued from a tavern urinal was the inheritor of one million bucks. I had trouble believing that, even though I knew zip about his past.

Then again, there must be some truth to the tale, otherwise why would a sophisticated and beautiful woman spend her time with a down-and-outer like yours truly? (Even though I had 'sensual' lips).

I followed Suzy Anger up the stairs, watching that beautiful fanny undulate in the mini-skirt. At the top I edged by her, taking a deep whiff of her seductive lilac and roses scent, fumbled for my key and opened the door.

The smell was like a hammer blow to the face.

Grandma Jones had taken me to a small slaughterhouse once and I had watched a man in a fenced-off pen lift a sledgehammer and bring it down in a vicious arc between the eyes of a horse that stood with lowered head, meekly submitting to the execution. The animal had collapsed in a heap and the man had gutted it with a razor-sharp half-moon blade. At the moment of death, the animal's guts had filled with gas and exploded with such force when the man pierced the skin with the knife that it knocked him backward. I'll never forget the stench that erupted from the horse's belly.

I smelled it many times in Viet Nam, cradling the bloody head of a buddy taken down by enemy fire, listening to him moan as his life force vacated his body, the whir of the Medivac chopper's blades overhead.

The putrid stench of violent death.

The smell that barreled headlong out of my open apartment door was the smell of that hammered, gutted horse. Of the men that died in my arms in 'Nam.

I gagged, reaching for the light switch and flooded the living room with one-hundred-fifty watt chiaroscuro. In my off hours, I had painted the room on canvas many times. There was my rose-colored wing-backed chair. My green sofa with the dimpled covering. My chipped and stained cherry wood coffee table, purchased at the Salvation Army (as were all my clothes and most of my furniture) for two dollars; and my threadbare reversible wool rug with the American eagle pattern in faded gold and federal blue.

Old Virgil was there, too.

Prone on the rug, blood-red stain on his chest patterned like a Rorschach test. I walked slowly to his prostrate form. I had seen many bullet wounds, some fatal, during my tour in Viet Nam and it looked like the old drunk had probably been dead before he hit the carpet. Although my head was a bit fuzzy from my recent mini drinking bout with Suzy Anger, it looked to me like the shot had neatly pierced his tired old heart.

"Ah, shit," I sighed. I began to kneel down to check for a pulse.

From behind me, Suzy Anger grabbed my arm and pulled me up. She took hold of both my arms and shook me violently. "What happened?" she demanded. There was an insane timbre in her voice. "It was *him* wasn't it? Don't lie to me!"

"Who are you talking about, lady?" I said as I peeled her fingers off my arms. "That's my only friend in the world laying there, bleeding on my carpet. Who killed him? Why?"

She responded by putting her arms around me and pulling me close, shoving her crotch into mine and grinding lasciviously. What man in his right mind could resist a come-on like that? With old Virgil dead on the floor below us, I planted a rough kiss on her mouth, reached into her blouse and fondled her firm breasts, rolling an erect nipple between finger and thumb. I could taste the whiskey and suds on her tongue as she reached between my legs and grabbed my crotch, fumbling for my fly. I reached down and helped her, hearing the sharp rasp of the zipper as it slid open. She shoved her hand inside, expertly kneading my manhood, feeling it grow rock-hard between her fingers.

You're a dirt bag, Johnny Jump, I thought. Making love with your dead friend stretched out on the floor. But it was my nether head that was doing the thinking for me now, with a single-mindedness of purpose that negated any moral qualms I might have had.

"Oh, yes," I moaned, nibbling at her ear lobe.

Suddenly she stiffened and pulled back, looking over my shoulder, wide-eyed in terror. "Angelo, no!" she said.

"What?" I asked, aroused and confused.

I heard a rough grunt behind me and the whoosh of something heavy swinging through the air just before it crashed down on my head.

The room burst in an explosion of stars and I dropped like I had been hit with a Joe Frazier left hook.

I heard her voice, as if in a drug-induced hallucination.

"You killed him, you stupid bastard!"

Fade to black.

PART TWO:
4:01 A.M. - 8 A.M.

I came to slowly, as if waking out of a long dream.

In fact, I had been dreaming. Of the night before. I had been laboring over a large oil painting of Virgil. He sat in one of my aluminum and vinyl kitchen chairs (I paint in my kitchen, and take all my meals out), outfitted in his ubiquitous wool sweater, both hands on the head of his cane, which he had planted firmly in front of him.

It was without doubt my best work. I had rendered him faithfully, with those starry, idealistic peepers; his sagging jowls and puckered gums; swooping Bob Hope proboscis with its bulbous tip like a shimmering maraschino cherry swimming in a Pink Lady cocktail.

"How long I got to sit here, Johnny?" he had asked, squirming in his chair.

"Not much longer, Virgil," I cautioned. "But sit still, please."

"I want a beer," he whined.

I was feeling that ultimate rush I could only receive when I was painting, and painting well. It was as if pure electricity coursed through my veins, and I had slipped into another, purer, world.

It had to be the same feeling that Pablo felt when he had painted "Guernica," or maybe one of the erotic renderings of his many mistresses. My man Pablo never let marriage get in the way of his love life.

The difference between Pablo and me, of course, was that his paintings sold for millions, and mine bartered for a month's rent at a time.

But the pure poetry of the act of creation was identical: the passionate rush, the ecstasy and joy.

The canvas was life-sized. I had placed Virgil on a flat black background and was slowly adding bright stars and planets, luminous comets, oranges and cherries suspended in the night sky. The world as he saw it.

I was daubing a speck of magnesium yellow in the center of a star when a rough knock on the door interrupted me. I continued painting, ignoring it. Virgil began to seriously squirm in his chair as the knocking continued unabated. Things were getting out of hand. I was losing the flow of the moment. I set the brush down at the side of the cheap dinner plate I used as a palette.

"There's beer in the fridge," I told Virgil as I left to answer the door. He slid off the chair and rushed to the Frigidaire.

"Don't drink all of them," I said over my shoulder as I opened the door.

Jesse Hardaway, owner of Jesse's tap, one door away from Ned's insurance agency on the street below, stood with hands on his hips.

"Ah'm gettin' sick an' tarred (Tired, he meant. Jesse is from Louisiana and has a Cajun accent you could slice with a knife. He was a friend of Grandma Jones back home, even though he is white, which is why he tolerates me.) of answerin' yer phone messages, boy," he said, thrusting a slip of paper into my hand. I have no phone, and those who need to urgently reach me (which is nearly nobody) call Jesse's and leave a message there.

"I wouldn'ta brung it up, 'cept it's from yer boss, an' he says he needs you now."

He turned and walked back down the steps, mumbling angrily, as I unfolded the note and read the summons from Sparky, grand poobah of Sparky's Cab Company, to report for work ASAP. Eddie Torrelli was with his wife in the hospital, who was giving birth to their seventh child. Sparky was short a driver and it was my turn to fill in.

Damned over-populating Catholics, I cursed under my breath. Hadn't they ever heard of birth control? It was Saturday night; my night to paint and drink and now I was going to have to drive late shift. Saturday night, when the beasts prowled and the chance of being robbed by a hopped-up junkie increased tenfold. I crumpled the note and threw it disgustedly on the floor. I wandered into the kitchen, where Virgil was taking sips from a cold can of Budweiser in between contented puffs from the left-over stub of a Dutch Masters Presidents cigar.

"I have to work, Virgil," I said. "Don't you drink all my beer." I clapped him on the shoulder.

"I won't, Johnny," he replied, looking up at me with his bulging, froggy eyes. His irises swam like green planets in a milk-white sky. Or they would have, if I could have continued painting.

"I got money, too, Johnny," he said, laying a trio of crumpled frog pelts on the Formica-topped table. "I'll buy a six-pack, huh?"

"You save that and get yourself some breakfast, pal. I'll bring a case home with me after work. We'll get back to work on the painting then, okay?"

"Sure, Johnny." A big tear formed in the corner of one eye. Virgil sometimes got uncomfortably maudlin.

"You're the only person who's ever been good to me, Johnny. God's gonna reward you someday."

"Hell, Virgil. Who else would pose for me the way you do? Look on all of this as just your pay for an honest day's work."

"Okay, Johnny." He sipped at the beer and puffed on the cigar, suddenly lost in the great, wonderful, exclusive world that existed behind his eyes.

It was the last time I saw him alive.

***

I grunted and slowly got up on one knee, shaking my head to clear it of cobwebs. I stood and stumbled to the sofa and collapsed onto it. How long had I been out?

The old Starr's Jeweler's clock (Starr's had gone out of business three years before, and I'd purchased the clock at a downtown rummage sale for fifty cents.) read four-oh-one A.M. I had entered the apartment with Suzy Anger just prior to three-thirty A.M. and it hadn't been very long after that I had been conked on the noggin, so I assumed that I'd been out for nearly thirty minutes.

Long enough for whoever it was to have absconded with the beautiful Suzy, as it seemed she had disappeared.

Also long enough to have bundled up old Virgil's corpse and carried it away.

At least, that's what must have happened, as there was no body on my American eagle rug.

And no blood stains.

If in fact I *had* seen the old man, shot through the heart, prostrate on my floor.

Maybe I had been dreaming all along. Maybe I had never gotten the note from Sparky, had never picked up Suzy Anger at the train station, had never seen Virgil sprawled on my rug, or been knocked on the head and left for dead.

It has happened more than once: a wild and prolonged bout with the bottle, passing out on my apartment floor. Waking with no memory of what had transpired the night before, and once waking with a chubby Mexican-American woman of sixty or more snoring loudly at my side. As I slid out of bed and pulled on my pants, I struggled to remember something, *anything* about the evening's revelries. Friends later stated I had been spotted in a variety of local saloons with not one but *three* geriatric senoritas of south-of-the-border ancestry; imbibing copious quantities of Cuervo Gold and singing "La Cucaracha."

That may have been true, (my friends have been known to lie when the occasion suits them) but to this day I still don't know how I ended up with that woman in my bed.

So perhaps *this* had all been a dream.

I struggled to my feet and walked to the kitchen and reached out to turn on the tap and run some cold water to splash on my face. It was then that I noticed my right hand was clenched into a fist. I opened it to reveal a crumpled slip of paper inside. I unfolded the paper and read the note that had been scribbled on it:

Johnny Jump—Go to Murderous Books in Milwaukee and ask for the owner, Sol Katzenberg. He can tell you more about these people and what they're capable of. I want to tell you more, but I can't. They're taking me away now, and my life is in danger.
Suzy Anger

There was a fleck of blood in one corner of the note, below the book store's address, punctuating the urgency of the message.

So it hadn't been a dream.

My aching head swam with unanswered questions:

Who was Suzy Anger, and was her story about Virgil inheriting a million dollars true?

Who had murdered Virgil (If he had indeed been killed), and where was his corpse?

Who was the "Angelo" she had called out to just before I had been conked on the noggin? Had he murdered Virgil?

Suzy had mentioned "these people" in her note. Who were they, and was her life in danger?

I checked the address on her note. It was near the University of Wisconsin-Milwaukee campus. After completing my tour in 'Nam at the end of nineteen-sixty-seven, I had spent a semester at the university auditing a class on English romantic poets but mostly sucking up beer and drugs with an endless array of hippies (pathetic middle-class kids who believed they were rebelling against society but were actually just making assholes of themselves, getting high and spouting Mao) in my digs just off Farwell and Brady streets. Trying to (and sometimes succeeding) score some hippie nookie.

It had been an off-the-wall, funky neighborhood with a lot of old-style, old-world character, and I hadn't been back there since nineteen-sixty-eight.

Had it changed, I wondered, in the ensuing five years?

I was going to find out, and soon. I hadn't had the opportunity to squander the forty-four bucks I had made on my Friday night shift, and my cab was parked outside with damned near a full tank of gas. I could make it to Murderous Books in forty-five minutes. I'd score breakfast and some coffee and wait around for the joint to open.

As I re-read the name Sol Katzenberg on Suzy's note, I fingered the Star of David I wore around my neck.

I'm a hodgepodge of persecuted minorities. My father's grandfather was a Polish Jew who spent the war years hidden in the basement of a sympathetic farmer while the Nazis murdered millions of his Jewish brethren in a rampage of systematic executions. Enraged and bent on revenge, he emerged from the basement in nineteen-forty-four and joined the Polish partisans, killing Nazis and wreaking havoc on their war machinery: an eye for an eye, real Old Testament stuff.

After the war, the Russians displayed their everlasting gratitude by tossing him in a camp in the Gulag; a god-forsaken hell-hole on the mainland off Sakhalin Island where he toiled sixteen hours a day chipping gold out of the frozen rock. He managed to escape, stowaway on a Liberian freighter and make his way first to Australia and then to America, where his brother, who had slipped out of Poland before the Nazi invasion, ran a tiny corner grocery store in Chicago.

I never met the man (he passed on when I was a baby) and I don't practice the religion, but I wear the Star as a symbol of my grandfather's great courage and will to survive.

Like Picasso: courage, the will to survive and to create. If this past night could be rendered onto canvas, I thought as I slowly closed my apartment door behind me and descended the steps to my cab below, it would be a masterpiece that would rival and perhaps even surpass "Guernica."

But some things just *are*. They cannot be translated onto canvas, or into a musical composition, or chiseled into marble.

Like my great-grandfather secreted in that dank basement, while the screams of the murdered Jews above echoed in his ears.

Like old Virgil on my carpet, black blood pooled on his threadbare rummage-sale sweater.

Like my trembling hands as I slid the keys into the ignition and started the cab.

***

As I pulled out of the alley and onto the street, I switched off the cab's radio. Once I was reported missing with the vehicle, Sparky would be huddled at the dispatcher's desk in the living room of his ranch-style brick home. I could envision him screaming into the mike while his Italian-born wife served him his supper of spaghetti and sausage, slathering butter on his Italian bread while banging away messages that I knew would increase in volume and fury as he searched for yours truly. No sense tempting fate by remaining accessible on the air.

I headed west toward the interstate. An occasional bread truck or other delivery vehicle passed me going in the opposite direction but other than that the streets were nearly deserted.

Except for the pair of headlights that remained in my rearview: bright yellow eyes that followed me onto 1-94 and north to Milwaukee.

I slowed and kept in the right lane, hoping the headlights would swerve around and pass me. No such luck. They remained behind, slowing down to a crawl when I did, accelerating in response as I pushed the cab faster.

No doubt about it. I was being tailed.

By who, I couldn't say. But I felt a sense of foreboding in those headlights, as if they should be blinking a warning in Morse Code.

Danger, Johnny Jump.

Turn back. Go home.

***

When Pablo was eight (or so the story goes), his father (an accomplished artist himself), recognizing the boy's genius, handed his paints and his brushes to his son and never again set paint to canvas, encouraging Pablo instead to accept the mantle of greatness that with which God had so obviously gifted him.

"If you become a soldier," his mother had told him. "You'll become a general. If you become a monk, you'll end up as the pope!"

Nothing like a little positive parental encouragement, huh? I envy Pablo his art, his mistresses, his place in the sun; but most of all I envy him his parents.

I used to think that if I had had supportive parents my life might have been dramatically different. It was probably true, and for a long time I carried a deep resentment in me because things were not as I imagined they should have been. Viet Nam changed that. Seeing your buddies dead in the elephant grass, torn by shrapnel and bullets, can skew your perspective on life. I believe now we are dealt one hand in life, and we play those cards as best we can.

But I still envy Picasso his mom and pop.

I was wondering what Sparky would do when he discovered I'd really gone missing with his cab. After a few hours of shouting into the dispatcher's mike, I believed he'd begin to worry. He knew me not to be a thief, so his natural conclusion would be to deduce that something evil had befallen me. Or that I had tied on a monumental drunk and was passed out in the cab in some forgotten alleyway.

There was no way I could call in to tell him my plans. For a number of reasons. First, Sparky would blow his stack. Cabs were for business, not personal ventures. There was no bending that rule, anytime, anywhere. Second, because I believed a man was murdered in my apartment, I was not eager to bring the cops down on me. Even if the body had disappeared. Even if I wasn't sure there *had* been a murder.

Third, I couldn't shake the image of the beautiful Suzy Anger. The rich, buttery smell of her perfume, her velvet lips surrendering to mine.

And the terrified look on her face as she glanced over my shoulder and spied whoever it was had slugged me.

She had even tried to warn me. "Angelo, no!" she had screamed.

Now she had been spirited away, was probably in great danger. And here I was, Johnny Jump, off to the rescue. Lancelot in search of Guinevere.

Hey, if the shoe fits, right?

***

The tail hugged me as I left the freeway on the Sixth Avenue exit and made my way downtown. Night gave way to dawn, and I squinted as I stared into my rearview, trying to get a glimpse of who was following me. No dice. I could only make out the shadow of a head, capped by a brimmed hat. From that I deduced my tail was a man, but nothing else.

Downtown Milwaukee had been slowly going to the dogs for years. Strip bars, porno book stores, sleazy ham and eggers; all competed for retail space in an area where even the most idealistic eye would see it was sliding downhill fast.

At five a. m. on a Sunday morning, the sidewalks and streets had a pale, ghostly visage. I would have liked to set up my easel smack in the middle of the main drag and render that image for posterity: the broad-shouldered buildings; the street lights winking green, yellow, red; spent night owls wandering aimlessly down the sidewalks like the pale ghosts of benders past.

I drove east down Wisconsin Avenue (followed by my tail, which I could now see was a bumble-bee-yellow nineteen-sixty-eight Dodge "Super Bee," a muscle car capable of overtaking my nineteen-sixty-nine Chevy Impala in a heartbeat, should I decided to try and shake him). Wisconsin Avenue dead-ended at Prospect, which swung north. The normally busy thoroughfare was nearly deserted as I zipped past newer high rises where secured doors and entryways offered a modicum of protection from the society's shabbier elements; turn-of-the-century ornate stone and leaded glass mansions that had been converted into rooming houses or the offices of real estate agents, doctors, lawyers and various other scam artists and tools of the establishment.

The sun peeked over the lake, tinting the sky with bright red-orange hues, carving broad shadows out of the buildings and homes. I shielded my eyes from the glare, again fixing my eyes onto my rearview. The Super Bee was still trailing me: my ghostly double; an unwanted *doppelganger*.

It was obvious I wouldn't shake him. He was going to hang on to me like a terminal disease.

I took a left at the Brady Street light and headed two blocks west, crossing Farwell and entering the former hippie haven I had called home for six months. Not out of nostalgic longing, but because I remembered there was George Webb's just down Brady Street, where you could get a cheeseburger, cup of coffee and fries any time of the day.

It wasn't yet six a.m., and I was positive Mr. Sol Katzenberg of Murderous Books, Inc. was not yet open for business.

Plenty of long hairs still cruised the streets, high on dope, and a few of the local saloons I remembered fondly were already open for business, (In violation of city law, but who the hell cared, as long as trouble confined itself to the frayed cuff and dirty collar neighborhoods?). I drove slowly by a bandy-legged drunk who conquered a tavern's ten-step concrete stoop like Edmund Hillary scaling Everest's summit.

There were still the few radical book stores, frayed posters calling for the end to the war in Viet Nam hanging by their edges from curling yellowed scotch tape in the dirty plate glass windows, stacked copies of the alternative *Bugle* newspaper on wide window sills littered with the mummified corpses of hundreds of flies. The rock n' roll shops offering the Beatles, Joplin, Hendrix, Morrison and the Doors; the dead or disbanded icons of a movement slowly losing both its steam and its idealism. Spider plants dangled from macramé plant holders that hung in every window and tie-dye dominated the second-hand clothing stores.

And everywhere those damned yellow smile faces!

Nothing had changed, yet everything had changed. There was a shabby, defeatist edge to the neighborhood; like a starlet in her middle years who gazes wistfully in the mirror one morning, and spying the wrinkles and amorphous, liquid sorrow in her eyes realizes she has squandered her youth and her beauty.

George Webb's was a Rock of Gibraltar in a neighborhood on its way toward radical and unpleasant change. I parked the cab curbside in front of the restaurant. My tail pulled around and sped past me, avoiding my stare as I strained to get a good view of who he was. All I saw was the back of his head, crowned by his hat. But by the spiral cord stretching from his hand to the dash, I deduced he was speaking into a hand-held mike like the one I used in my cab. Whoever it was following me was not operating alone. He had a radio in his car and a base command, which meant he was reporting my movements. Which also meant that more than one person was interested in where I was going. Suzy Anger was my main concern now, so my discovery of who they were and what their purpose was would have to wait. The yellow Dodge turned a corner and disappeared from view as I sauntered inside the greasy spoon.

The predictable Saturday night drunks were crowded at the counter, scarfing down bacon and eggs and sloshing coffee on the Formica. The cursing waitress who served this motley crew and policed their messes could have stepped right out of Les Demoiselles d'Avignon. She had an unsettling, Picasso-like, out-of-kilter face and makeup that looked like she had applied it in a spastic fit. Her cherry-red lipstick absently wandered away from her thick lips and her harshly-plucked eyebrows swept up at the ends like two black wings attempting to spirit away her nose.

"Wha' chew want?" she asked as I wedged myself between a long-hair and a hard hat; both drunk, both fumbling with knife and fork.

"Cheeseburger," I said. "And fries."

Her eyebrows flapped as she frowned. "It's breakfast."

"It's cheeseburgers," I retorted. Hell if I was going to allow her to push me around.

"Asshole," she mumbled as she tossed a graying hamburger patty on the griddle. The meat sizzled and spit fat as it hit the hot metal.

"Lucky ain't got much of a personality for dealing with the public," said the hard hat on my right.

"But she sure can burn them eggs," said the hippie on my left, grimacing as he speared a forkful of leathery yolk and runny white.

"Lucky?" I asked the hippie.

"Her name's actually Louise but we all call her Lucky 'cause she hates it so much," said the hard hat. I noticed he sported a tiny gold hoop earring in one ear and a wispy Fu Manchu mustache. He removed the hard hat and placed it on his lap. His head had been shaved bald. In fact, if his earring had been a bit larger, and he'd shaved the mustache, he would have been a dead ringer for Mr. Clean.

He noticed my curious stare and ran a hand over his naked crown. "Saves on the haircuts," he said, grinning.

"I bet."

"Sol has sold out to the Man," said the hippie. "Abandoned the revolution."

"What revolution?" asked the hard hat. "The peace agreement in Viet Nam's been inked, and that takes all the wind out of your sails, Harvey. Without the war, you've got no revolution. None of you do."

"Sol?" I asked the hard hat.

"The revolution's more than the war. It's a state of mind. It's equity and justice and freedom," said the hippie.
He lifted his chin slightly in an obnoxious, self-righteous gesture.

"Can the political patter, Harv," said the hard hat. "The draft's been suspended. Your ass is safe for now."

I liked his take-no-prisoners style as he put the self-righteous hippie in his place, so when Hard Hat lifted a hand for me to shake, I took it.

"Sol Katzenberg," he said. "Proprietor of Murderous Books, Inc."

"I don't believe it," I said. "I came up here looking for you."

"For me?" he said in mild surprise. A cloud of suspicion brewed in his stare.

"You're not a narc, are you? I'm clean. Been that way for three years." Studying my shaggy coiffure and patchwork clothing ensemble, he said, "No, of course you're not; but these days anyone could be undercover."

I handed him Suzy Anger's note. As he read it, his mouth opened slightly in mild astonishment.

"I think my friend has been murdered," I said as he looked up from the note and into my eyes. "An old man who wouldn't have harmed anyone. And somebody has kidnapped the woman who wrote this note."

"You're in great danger," he said, mouthing the words slowly in a theatrical manner. "They could be watching you this very minute."

He glanced furtively around the busy diner, searching for suspicious faces.

Feeling as if I was trapped in a schlocky b-movie *film noir*, I cut to the chase. "In danger from whom?" Always with the proper English, me.

"Dark forces," he replied. "Evil men."

The whole situation was beginning to get a bit melodramatic and I was in the process of telling him so when two men with nylon stockings yanked over their faces burst through the front door. One leveled a sawed-off shotgun at the patrons, the other a pistol with a taped handle at the waitress.

"Okay, bitch," commanded the man with the pistol. "Hand over the money!"

Lucky reached under the counter and came up with a Colt Python .357. Her hand shook as she pointed the cannon at the robbers.

"Eat lead, fuckers," she said, and pulled the trigger. The explosion shattered the silence as Sol Katzenberg pulled me by the arm and we (Along with all the drunks, who had suddenly gone sober) hit the floor.

The robbers responded in kind, and for a brief minute the restaurant reverberated with the echoes of a full-blown gun battle. Pots and pans flew as they were struck by errant bullets, clanking like an off-key futuristic symphony.

When the smoke cleared, the robber with the sawed-off shotgun lay dead on the floor and the other had fled empty-handed, dropping his pistol in the doorway.

Unhit and unharmed, the Python dangling from her hand, Lucky set the gun on the counter and dug a filterless cigarette and book of matches out of her apron pocket.

Fingers quivering nervously she lit up, puckered her lips and blew a solitary smoke ring that dissipated as it drifted toward the ceiling. She set the coffin nail on the counter's edge and returned to her work on the grill.

"I been robbed twice at gunpoint. I ain't gonna be robbed no more. Who had the cheeseburger?" she asked, nonchalantly flipping my patty.

Rising on one knee, Sol Katzenberg patted me on the shoulder. "It is time we exit this place. Pronto."

Nimbly dodging the robber's corpse (and the puddle of blood oozing out from under him) stretched out on the floor, I followed Sol Katzenberg out the door as police sirens echoed in the distance.

***

Murderous Books, Inc. was nestled in a commercial block building between an "art" shop offering uninspired "sofa-sized" landscapes (An insult to true art) and a bakery with a window counter filled with chocolate-covered long johns, cinnamon Danish and sugar-coated Bismarcks. I had a friend from New York tell me once that the best way to tell if a person was from the Chicago-Milwaukee corridor was if he called a jelly donut a Bismarck.

"It's a goddamned *jelly donut,* for chrissakes!" he'd said. "You people are weird, you know that?"

I retaliated by making a disparaging comment about the Mets. That's how you hurt New Yorkers; insult their sports teams. They're impervious to everything else. Denigrate wife, family, their litter-ridden streets and they shrug it off. But state that the Knicks are a limp-wristed bunch of sissies, or the Yankees couldn't hit their way out of a paper bag, and you've got a fight on your hands.

Sol Katzenberg fished a key ring out of his pocket, singled one out and shoved it into the lock of the old oak door to his book store. The key ring jingled as he turned the lock and pushed the door open.

Less than fifteen minutes earlier I had been hugging the floor of a burger joint while a violent shoot-out raged a few feet from me, but it seemed as if it had happened in another life, another time. It was the same with 'Nam. It was as if the kid (me) who hid under his helmet during mortar barrages, or fired blindly into the jungle where he thought the enemy lay in ambush was another person, some anti-hero I'd read about in a paperback novel.

I'm not too proud to admit I'd been terrified during much of my tour in Southeast Asia, but I came out tougher than when I went in; willing to kill to save my own ass, and the asses of those in my platoon. From the grunt's eye view, that's how you slice it in wartime. It's you and your buddies. Everything beyond that is superfluous. Keep yourself and those close to you out of harm's way, and kill the enemy. Anybody who tells you war is any more than that is full of shit.

The store smelled musty, stale; like what you'd expect in King Tut's tomb; was narrow, maybe twelve feet wide; and long, stretching back at least forty feet. The tunnel-like quality was enhanced by the floor-to-ceiling bookshelves that lined the walls, stuffed with old paperbacks and dog-eared hard covers. I picked a novel off one of the shelves. Its lurid magenta and lemon-yellow cover featured a busty blonde tied to a chair. The straps on her fire-engine-red evening gown clung tenuously to her shoulders, threatening to drop and expose her milk-white breasts. A man's long shadow ominously cast itself over the girl and onto the pock-marked wall behind her. Her eyes bulged in terror as they transfixed themselves onto the unseen evil presence behind the shadow.

"That's good stuff," said Sol Katzenberg, motioning to the book in my hand. "I've got all the greats in here: Hammett, Chandler, Jim Thompson, James M. Cain. You mark my words; in twenty years the mystery field's going to be filled with writers trying to copy those guys, and none of them will be nearly as good. I'm at the cutting edge of the trend."

"Maybe you haven't hit the 'edge' part yet," I said, noticing the thick dust that coated the books on the shelves. I also noticed he had suddenly lost the exaggerated drunken demeanor he'd exhibited at George Webb's.

He grunted. "That's always been my talent. Anticipate the future." He rubbed the hard hat as if he were trying to summon a genie. "Like my chapeau here."

He waved me on toward the back of the store. "C'mon, I've got something to show you."

As I followed him past the shelves he removed the hard hat and set it next to an antique National Cash Register on the high wooden counter at the rear of the store. I placed the novel with the lurid cover next to his hat and took the bar stool at the front of the counter (A natural perch for a lounge lizard like me).

He aimed a finger at the hat. "That signals to the aging 'revolutionaries' that I am no longer part of their movement; that I don't buy into their act anymore. They're pathetic and passé and don't even realize it."

"But you still wear the badges," I said, motioning to the mustache and earring.

"These," he replied, fingering the Fu Manchu and then the golden hoop, "Are mere vanity. I like the way they look. You know what's happening in this neighborhood? The same as in the Haight in San Francisco. The peace and love is long gone. Drugs have taken over. Scumbags with guns control these neighborhoods now. Soulless bastards. They hook runaways on heroin. Pimp out little girls. Kill for trivialities."

He dismissed his argument with a flick of his hand. "Ah, but what do I know?"

Retiring to a bar stool behind the counter he unfolded Suzy Anger's crumpled note. Concern lined his face as he reread it.

"Who are 'these people?'" I asked him. "Who is Suzy Anger?"

"You don't know?" He set the note on the counter and smoothed it out with the flat of his hand.

"Look. I'm a cabby. I take a fare to my apartment, walk in to find my roommate dead on the floor. I get hit on the head and wake up to find the fare gone, the body gone and nary a trace of both."

"'Nary a trace,'" he chuckled, mimicking me. "You seem too literate to be a cabby."

"Yeah. I'm goddamned *Shakespeare*, that's what. Tell me what in the hell is going on."

"You really don't know?" His eyes were flat and impassive. You're lying, they said. You know something, everything, and you're playing a game.

"I really don't." I was growing angry. Piss on him, I thought. Piss on his untrusting eyes.

"Okay, hot dog. I'll give you the whole story."

He took a deep breath and blew air out slowly. "In nineteen-fifty-two, the bodies of three little boys were found in a field in a township north of Chicago."

"I remember that," I said. "The Potter boys."

He nodded in assent. "Three brothers, sons of a wealthy black Chicago financier who'd made his fortune selling insurance to the blacks who migrated to Chicago from the deep south during the Depression. Ten, eleven and twelve years old. They'd been raped, tortured and then strangled."

"I didn't know they'd been sexually assaulted."

"No one did. The press and the police kept mum about it. It was too gruesome for that time. Nowadays . . ." he shrugged his shoulders, completing the statement with the gesture.

"The boys' parents naturally went into shock. The grief-stricken mother killed herself six months after. The father took longer, drinking himself to death over a period of five years, losing most of his fortune in the process."

He paused, and we sat in stony silence for a full minute before he began again.

"What do you know about your roommate, the old man who <u>called</u> himself Virgil?"

His eyes had become deep, fathomless pools. Like a crystal ball, I read what was at their center.

"No," I said. "Virgil wasn't capable of that. He was a harmless old man. A nobody."

"So *you* say. We knew the murder of the Potter boys had been perpetrated by someone close to the family, someone who knew the boys. Someone they trusted."

"How can you tie Virgil in to any of this?"

"Virgil was Potter's accountant," he said. "Only his name then was Robert Sampson. He disappeared the day the boys' bodies were found."

"Suzy Anger?" I asked, stunned by the revelation that the homeless old gent I took in may have been a murderer and pedophile.

"Sampson's daughter."

My jaw must have dropped, because I had trouble mouthing the words.

"His *daughter*?" I asked, remembering how she had come on to me like a runaway sexual freight train while the old man lay dead on the floor. "That can't be."

"But it is."

"She told me he had inherited a million dollars, and that she was his niece."

"Suzy's always been a liar, but the story about the money is partly true. After Robert Sampson disappeared, Potter discovered that the accountant had embezzled a million dollars over a period of five years. And the money and the man were now missing. Potter had trusted Sampson implicitly. Now his boys were murdered and defiled and his fortune had been plundered."

"You mentioned 'we' a few moments ago. Who are you? And who is 'we?'"

"My associates and I were hired by Max Potter to find Robert Sampson and bring him to justice. We were directed to do unto him what he had done to the boys. An eye for an eye."

"What are you, a bounty hunter?"

"That, and other things."

He reached over and fingered the Star of David hanging from my neck. "You're Jewish?"

"My great-grandfather was."

"Then you should understand what I'm talking about. Remember Susan Degnan?"

"Sure. Who doesn't? Little six year old girl who was found dismembered in a trash barrel. Nineteen-forty-six, wasn't it?"

"That's right. Another celebrated Chicago case. William Heirens, the girl's murderer, received life in prison. Max Potter didn't want that to happen to Robert Sampson. My associates and I guaranteed that when Sampson was found, he would suffer greatly before he was killed."

"You said Potter died in nineteen-fifty-seven. Why pursue Sampson for so long after?" I wasn't ready to admit Virgil was an embezzler, murderer and pedophile. Nor could I believe that anybody, no matter how dedicated, would follow up on a contract after the principal party was dead. You might chase down somebody in those circumstances because of love or family but never for money, especially after the money had been paid. The scenario smelled, but I kept my lips buttoned, and let him continue with his charade.

"We pursue, Johnny. We had been paid. Whether or not Potter was alive didn't matter. We always finish the job.

"We thought we'd cornered him a couple of times. He'd moved around a lot. South America, Europe, and then back here. He always seemed to stay a step ahead of us. He was spotted here on Brady Street about two years ago. I went into disguise as a long-hair, tried to ferret him out, but he had disappeared."

"Long hair?" I pointed to his shaved head.

"The chrome dome and hard hat are a recent phenomenon. I'm making a statement before I leave this place. I told you what's happening to this neighborhood. These Brady Street people are in for a hard fall. Their 'revolution,' as they like to call it, has failed. In fact, it never was. It was a collective figment of the imagination; an unattainable never-never land."

"A lot of them would argue with that."

"Let them. It won't change things."

"You're folding your tent, then?"

"Not until my mission is accomplished."

"It is, isn't it? Virgil . . . Sampson, is dead."

"Is he?"

"I saw him, dead on my floor."

"Then where is the corpse?"

"I thought you would know that."

He shook his head slowly. "Not me. Not anyone I work with. We searched your apartment and came up empty. No traces of blood. No signs of violence."

"You were in my place? When?"

"Before you woke from your assault."

I imagined myself unconscious on my floor while nameless men rummaged through my apartment. It pissed me off, and I felt the blood rush to my head.

"Why were you there? Who hit me on the head?"

"Who hit you? I don't know. But one of my associates wrote the note, pricked his finger with a pin and flicked blood on it. I thought it was bit melodramatic, but it worked. As far as why we were there; well, we were hunting an evil man, Johnny. All's fair in love and war, pal."

"Says you. How did you know I'd be at the restaurant?"

"I *anticipated* you, Mr. Jump. It's my talent. We know more about you than you realize. You're very predictable."

"I had a tail following me all the way up here. Was that one of your people?"

The corner of his lip twitched slightly. "You were followed? By who?"

"I'm asking you that."

"It wasn't one of us."

"Who are you people? Where is Suzy Anger?"

"Why don't you ask her yourself?"

He opened a door directly behind the counter, revealing a small room behind, barren of furniture with the exception of a single straight-backed wooden chair in the center of the room. A nude Suzy Anger sat bound to the chair with a series of interconnected electrical cords, one end of which was plugged into a naked outlet, the other which ended in a plug dangling at the base of the chair. A filthy rag had been shoved into her mouth, and her head bobbed like one of those ridiculous toy dogs on springs you see lolling about in the backs of station wagons filled with screaming kids. A bare bulb suspended overhead lit the room garishly, casting her distended shadow on the wall behind her.

Infuriated, I gripped the edge of the counter. "What the hell is this?"

A wolfish grin lit Sol Katzenberg's face.

"You see that plug on the floor? You're going to tell us everything you know, otherwise I'm going to take that rag out of her mouth and shove the plug in. Barbecue her beautiful ass."

"You cold-hearted, worthless piece of shit. Untie her."

"First a little information. Where's the money, Johnny Jump?"

"I don't know what you're talking about."

"The one million dollars your roommate stole from my client. Where is it?"

Teeth clenched, I said, "Let her go, or I'll kill you." I meant it.

He was unimpressed by my threat. "First the money."

I walked around behind the counter, angrily shoving Sol Katzenberg aside.

"What the hell do you think you're doing?" he said as I slammed him up against the wall.

"Untying her, of course."

I began to unfasten the thick knot that secured her to the chair. There were bruises on her breasts and thighs, where the cords had cut deeply into her skin. I took the rag out of her mouth, and she began to mumble.

"What?" I said, leaning closer in an effort to hear what she was saying,

"Father Abelard," she mumbled. "Find him." Spittle trickled from the corner of her mouth.

Powerful arms pinned my arms behind me. A pungent rag was shoved in my face. I recognized the smell. When I was seven years old I had had an operation to remove a cyst on my right ankle, and they'd used ether to put me under.

I struggled to free myself, involuntarily sucking in deep draughts of the drug. Just as had happened when I was seven and about to go under the doctor's knife, a maelstrom whirled about in my brain, sucking in my consciousness. Clouds furrowed in the room, smothering the light. I had a last glimpse of Suzy Anger, attempting to wriggle out of her bonds. I went limp and sank to the floor.

As I drifted into oblivion, I heard a voice that wasn't Sol Katzenberg's say "Leave him here. Untie the girl and dress her."

Fade to black, again.

The chair was splayed out like a wooden four-legged spider. The electrical cord at its feet curled like a snake around the discarded rag used to muffle Suzy's cries.

I was conscious of the fact of who I was, and where I was; but when I attempted to stand I sank back to the floor in defeat.

I waited until the heavier effects of the ether wore off, then stood on drunken legs and surveyed the empty room.

Nothing.

I wobbled out of the room and made a perfunctory search of the bookstore and also found nothing. Suzy, Katzenberg and even the hard hat had disappeared. Like the scene at my apartment earlier, it was as if they had never been there.

I exited Murderous Books, Inc. and staggered into the adjacent bakery, in search of a sucrose and caffeine fix to combat the lingering effects of the ether. I ordered an extra-large coffee and saucer-sized sugar cookie. The girl behind the counter had her hair twisted into French braids and a bright red "Impeach Nixon" button pinned to her white blouse. She added cream and sugar to my paper cup coffee and brown-bagged the cookie.

"If they impeach Tricky Dick, you realize Gerald Ford will be President?" I said as I pointed to her button. Ever the editorialist, me.

She looked at me with vapid blue eyes. "Anybody's better than Nixon."

She handed me the coffee and cookie.

"Not hardly." I paid her a buck for my food and drink.

"I dig your bandana," she said.

"Groovy," I replied, flashing the *V* for peace sign. Another young life on its way to nowhere, I thought as I exited the bakery.

But then I should talk, right?

I stood on the street corner outside the bakery, sipping coffee and munching on the cookie while I found my sea legs. I debated on my success thus far. Success was perhaps the wrong word. Bumbling may have been a better choice. I had exhibited the effectiveness of a retarded kindergartener in my search for Suzy Anger.

But I did have a clue to her whereabouts.

She had mumbled the name of Father Abelard as I attempted to untie her. The notorious priest and rabble-rouser was well-known to me. I had participated in one of his civil rights marches in the late sixties, and I knew he was still headquartered in a near west side coffee house run by the local chapter of the Black Panthers.

I ate the last of the cookie, brushing crumbs and sugar granules off my shirt and downed the coffee, tossing the paper cup and brown bag into a nearby trash receptacle. A sign on the side of the can read "Keep Milwaukee Clean." Trash lay strewn on the sidewalk all around it. Save the earth, baby. It looked like the latest hippie mantra was having limited effect locally.

The cab coughed as I started it, jerking away from the curb as if it were reluctant to continue our *anabasis*.

"I don't blame you, old girl," I said, gently patting the dash. "I feel the same way; but we've got to finish what we've started."

I drove up Prospect, then west, passing Hooligan's Super Bar, one of my favorite watering holes when I lived in the area. Draft beers then were ten cents and shots were twenty cents. I relished working on cheap drunks, munching Blind Robins; the dried, salted, packed in plastic fish whose pungent odor rivaled that of limburger cheese as I engaged in animated conversation with one or more of the outlandish menagerie that called Hooligan's home.

I still had a Kelly green and white Hooligan's t-shirt buried in a dresser drawer somewhere. The last time I had worn it was under a corduroy sport coat on a blind date to Frenchy's restaurant, where exotic wild game was a menu staple. I had ordered Bengal Tiger steak and a salad of flower petals. My date (I can't recall what she looked like, only that she had had the disgusting habit of vegetarianism and spent most of our brief encounter trying to convert me) had made a sour face and walked out.

Nonplused, I devoured the meat with gusto, remembering the tiger that had pounced into a trench in 'Nam that I had occupied with other GIs and a few ARVN Rangers. The beast had torn out the throat of a shrieking Ranger and we had emptied three full clips into it before it collapsed and died.

I remembered that brutal scene as I savored the meat. Maybe I was chewing on that tiger's brother or sister. Payback time.

"Karma, Mr. Tiger," I'd mumbled as I ate.

Someday, I'd return to Milwaukee with my sometime girlfriend/model Jennifer in tow and do the city up right. After I'd sold a painting for some real money, maybe.

But the hell with all of that now.

Picasso once said, "I do not seek, I find."

I was going to seek and find Suzy Anger, and confront those who had probably murdered my friend, kidnapped my fare and twice put me under.

It had been one hell of a long day.

And it was only eight o'clock in the morning.

PART THREE
8:01 A.M. - NOON

In art, Pablo was always the rebel. But in social status, he strove to reach the top; the crème de la crème. He had no problem hobnobbing with the idle rich, realizing they were the men and women who bought his paintings and fawned over him as if he were some sort of god. The men envied him, the women worshipped him, and both threw money at him.

"Rebel" had been a word often associated with Father Abelard. In the late nineteen-sixties he had led a series of anti-war marches on the state capitol in Madison, through Milwaukee and even into downtown Chicago. The marchers were met with police riot sticks and tear gas; and Father Abelard was pressured by the church to give up his crusade. Things will change in their own way and in their own time, he was told.

He not only disobeyed the orders of his superiors, he went public with their communiqués. He was excommunicated for his efforts but he refused to remove his frock, stating that the Church had become corrupt and the tool of big money interests and therefore had no authority over the true followers of Christ.

Well la-dee-da, I remembered thinking at the time he had made that statement. And where were you in seminary, on the moon? Or didn't you realize what had happened to St. Francis, Galileo and scores of others who found themselves at odds with the Church?

I didn't begrudge the good Father his principles. It's just that I've discovered over the years that principles (in everything excluding art, of course) have created more problems than they've cured. I don't knock religion. I believe; but not in the bricks-and-mortar, praise-Jesus-and-pass-the-collection-plate-faith practiced by most everyone else. Just so you know my position on the matter, and we'll let it stand at that.

The Inasmuch Coffee House was located at Nineteenth and Highland, in the western fringe of an area that any dummy could see was poised to become a full-blown, Chicago-style ghetto. There wasn't a white face to be seen the last six blocks before the coffee house, which occupied a tired blue frame structure of the type so common in Milwaukee. A man I befriended in my college days (a prodigious beer drinker who had a peculiar fondness for pork rinds) called them "the workingman's castle;" neat, two-story clapboard houses with a small front porch and narrow yard behind.

In other areas of Milwaukee these homes sat shoulder to shoulder on immaculate side streets filled with rosy-cheeked kids playing ball, jumping rope and riding bikes while mom busied herself with her rose bushes as supper bubbled happily
on the stove, and dad lounged on the porch after work, sipping beer, scanning the evening *Journal*. A blue-collar *Leave it to Beaver* world.

Not in *this* neighborhood.

I knew the area well. It had once been the haunt for the local Black Panthers. A few of my more radical hippie girlfriends had coerced me into attending meetings. Though why these lily-white suburban girls slavered over people who preached death to those of European ancestry, I'll never know. The Panthers accepted their obsequiousness, sexual favors and dollars while exhibiting open contempt for them. Those were the days of Fred Hampton, Mark Clark, Huey Newton and people like Ron Uhuru, leader of the American Pan-Africa Movement. Many said Uhuru was instrumental in fomenting the nineteen sixty-seven Watts riots. I had witnessed Uhuru deliver an impassioned speech promising violent eradication of the white race at the University of Wisconsin-Milwaukee campus. At the end of his speech, the Caucasian cognoscenti (more than half the audience) jumped up and gave the man a standing ovation.

I remained seated (ignoring the judgmental frowns of the effete professorial pantywaists enthusiastically applauding at either side of me). I wasn't about to clap for a man who promised to rub out the white, red, yellow, black or any other race. What would he do with somebody like me? Slaughter my white side, and spare the black?

Putting away unpleasant memories, I parked the cab at the curb in front of the Inasmuch Coffee House.

The houses on either side of the coffee house had been torched in the nineteen sixty-eight riots that followed Martin Luther King's assassination when Milwaukee, like scores of other big cities, teetered on the edge of all-out rebellion. A dawn to dusk curfew had been imposed, and police prowlers crawled along the streets in great numbers. A few snipers had traded shots with the cops and three (snipers, not cops) had been killed. The houses had never been rebuilt, leaving Abelard's headquarters flanked by two litter-strewn empty lots.

The coffeehouse sported American flags for curtains and peeling paint on the clapboards. A gaggle of black kids mingling on the scruffy front lawn slowly split as I made my way to the front door, which I opened. A bead curtain separated the interior of the home from the small foyer. I parted it (like Moses) and walked inside.

The first floor had been gutted to create one large room, which held a half dozen tables and accompanying chairs scattered without rhyme or reason over the bare plank floor. A small table with a percolator coffee pot and stacked mugs (along with the tables and chairs) was the only indicator that this was indeed a public house.

The walls were festooned with posters of Che Guevera, Malcom X, Eldridge Cleaver, Mark Clark, Fred Hampton, Ho Chi Minh, Mao and other icons of the "movement." Looking misplaced among the political mishmash was a large photo of recently deceased Grateful Dead band member James "Pig Pen" McKernan, in stars and stripes bonnet, bushy mustache and goatee. It had been less than a month since McKernan had succumbed to the effects of his suicidal drinking habit, liver annihilated by cirrhosis. Another soldier who gave his life for rock n' roll.

Seeing no one and hearing no one, I poured myself a cup of coffee and took a seat. Grandma Jones had taught me that it was always best to "wait and see what the other fella had t' say befo' you open yo' own mouth." I was doing just that when the bead curtain that separated the public area from the rest of the house parted and two wiry black men in 'fros, impenetrable shades and black tams strode into the room. They wore army-issue jackets and khaki pants and the bulges in their pockets sent a clear signal that both were packing.

They strode in lockstep, diverging as they neared the table; one standing at my left, the other at my right; both with crossed arms, like twin ebony lawn ornaments.

The one on my left, who wore a Leroi Jones-style mustache and goatee, opened his mouth to reveal less than perfect teeth.

"You lookin' for someone?" he asked. The tone in his voice clearly implied, 'Get your ass out. Now.'

"Thought I'd have a cup of coffee," I replied.

"No one comes here for coffee," interjected the second, stating the obvious.

"I can see that," I said, scoping the empty room. "How about some conversation, then?"

"What kind of 'conversation?'" Number One asked.

"I'm looking for Father Abelard."

Number One flinched and made a feint for the bulge in his pocket.

I held up a cautionary hand. "Take it easy. I'm not the enemy."

Number Two lifted his shades to reveal piercing burnt umber eyes. Looking me over, he asked "You a brother?"

"Part of me is. My mother was half black."

"You half-ass then," hissed Number One. "You don't belong anywhere. Not black. Not white."

"You'll have to excuse my brother," said Number Two in perfect King's English. "He takes great exception to the mongrelization of the races."

"Father Abelard?" I asked again, ignoring the racist diatribe.

Number One's hand slid closer to the bulge in his pocket. "Father don't want to see you. Maybe you come to do him harm?"

"Not hardly. I need his help. I have to tell you, this is becoming a very unpleasant experience."

"Not as unpleasant as what's gonna happen to you if you don't haul your half-black ass outta here right now," said Number One.

"You seem to have gotten yourself in a rather sticky situation," said Number Two, flashing a mouthful of gold-capped teeth.

"Very sticky," I mugged, blowing him a kiss. The grin fled his face, and he stepped back, scowling as he held clenched fists at his sides.

"Dead meat, half-ass," hissed Number One, pulling a short-barreled thirty-eight out of his jacket pocket.

"Slow down," commanded a voice from behind. Five diminutive digits thrust themselves between the bead curtain and opened it, revealing the defrocked Father Abelard. He was smaller than I imagined him to be. Stoop-shouldered, and with a tired expression on his lined face, he wore a thin gray sweater under a corduroy sport jacket, blue jeans and worn brown penny loafers. A cigarette dangled from his thin lips, trailing smoke behind him as he shuffled across the floor. He pulled out a chair, sat and stared at me from across the table. Gone was the look of fierce defiance I had remembered from the press photos I had seen in the middle and late nineteen-sixties. It had been replaced with a world-weary, untrusting sorrow.

"What can I do for you?" he asked, setting two paperbacks on the table; *The Communist Manifesto* and an abridged copy of Darwin's *Origin of the Species*. As a kid, I didn't remember my Catholic school pals studying out of either.

"Father Abelard? I'm looking for Sol Katzenberg." I asked.

Abelard reached into his pocket and pulled out an orange. He slid his thumb under its skin and skillfully peeled it, the peel curling in one long unbroken spiral as it fell to the tabletop. He broke the orange in two and removed a wedge, delicately bit into it, chewed slowly and swallowed.

"Sol proved to be one of the major disappointments of my life," he said. "I trusted the man, and he betrayed me. He was a tool of the military-industrial complex. I should have seen it, but I didn't."

'Me,' I noticed he said. Not 'us,' or 'the cause.' 'Me.' Maybe the good Father suffered from a Christ complex.

"Why do you want Sol?" Abelard asked, popping another orange wedge into his mouth.

"Don't tell him nothin'. He's a cop," said Number One, pointing an accusatory finger at me.

""He doesn't have cop's eyes," said Father Abelard.

He turned his gaze back on me and for a second I thought I saw a flash of his old hypnotic power.

"You're no cop, are you, Mr. . ."

"Johnny Jump."

Number One snickered. "What the hell kind of half-ass name is that?"

I had had it with them. "Go to hell," I said.

The tension in the room sizzled like bacon in the pan.

"You and Mohammed leave us, please Kareem," asked Father Abelard politely.

"Father," said Mohammed. "Mr. Johnny Jump is no gentleman."

"On the contrary, I was raised to mind my manners, unlike two uncultured assholes I know," I shot back.

"Later, man," warned Hakeem. The two lingered menacingly at the doorway before disappearing behind the bead curtain.

The priest breathed a sigh of relief after they left.

"I've lost control of those two, I'm afraid," he said.

"I'm surprised you keep them around, Father, considering their politics. You being white, and all." It was a snotty comment, and he knew it.

"We are all God's children. One in the same."

"Even a mongrel like me?"

He smiled patronizingly. "Even you."

"Well then bless you Father, for your Christian charity. I only wish your followers exhibited the same tolerance."

"Some people just hate. They don't know the reason why. Hakeem and Mohammed are that way. Don't take what they say personally. It just a . . ." he searched for the right word. ". . . reflex action, that's all."

"One of them pointed a rather large pistol in my direction. If he would have shot me, would *that* have been a reflex action, Father?"

"He never would have pulled the trigger. I trust him."

Sure, *you* trust him, he shoots *me*, I thought.

"Now," he said. "Why do you want Sol?"

Studying his unimpressive appearance, I wondered why so many had poured their hearts out to this man, laid bare sins and weaknesses, and followed Abelard to hell and back. I surely never would, I thought.

But being of a more practical nature, I chose instead to tell the story of what had transpired from the time I'd picked Suzy Anger up at the train station. It was a matter of finding myself at a dead end, with no place else to go. I felt it was dangerous to confide in him, but I had to have a lead. I couldn't shake the image of Suzy Anger, hog-tied to that chair; drugged, mumbling incoherently.

He calmly sipped at his coffee, puffing on his cigarette as I poured out my story. The half-eaten orange lay forgotten on the table. Shimmering droplets of juice sparkled on the worn mahogany.

"Have you ever heard of the Deutschland Athletic Association?" he asked.

I shook my head in the negative.

"It's where you probably could find Sol," said the priest.

"Where do I find this place?"

"I wouldn't be so hasty, Johnny. The Deutschland Athletic Association is a front for local Nazis."

"So what would a man named Katzenberg being doing in a joint like that?"

"Good question. If the man you met this morning was the real Sol Katzenberg, that is. Sol Katzenberg died in Chicago in 1968, during the Democratic convention riots. Some say it was the direct result of a police nightstick on the head, but it can't be proved."

"Then who was the man in the bookstore?"

"My sources say he's Ernst Von Schulte, a dedicated Jew-baiter and a man who excels in race hatred."

He lit a second cigarette off the first and inhaled deeply. "I met him in 1971, in an anti-war march. The cops had been infiltrating our organization for years, but they'd been clumsy, and their moles were easy to spot. Not Sol Katzenberg. He was as smooth as they come, and I'm embarrassed to say he took me in."

"He was working for the police?"

"No. And as near as I can tell, he wasn't working for the Deutschland Athletic Association, either. A loner. Someone impossible to pigeonhole, and therefore the most dangerous kind of man."

Confused, I asked, "What did he want?"

"I was hoping you could tell me."

"I told you everything I know."

His look said he thought I had held something back. "That he was a detective, working on a murder case? Do you believe that?"

"I believe some of it must have been true. But I don't believe what he said about old Virgil."

"That he murdered the Potter boys? It's plausible."

"Barely."

"I agree." He leaned forward and tapped the back of my hand with a skinny finger. I noticed his nicotine-stained nails were bitten to the nub.

"I'll tell you something," he whispered, glancing at the beaded curtain behind us, where Kareem and Mohammed had disappeared. "Trust nobody in this world. *Nobody.*"

He leaned back in his chair and cupped his hands behind his head. I spied the slight bulge under his right armpit, and I realized good Father Abelard was wearing a shoulder holster. What Catholic order did he belong to? Not that it mattered. I was pretty sure pistol packing had not been an integral component of Christ's teachings.

"Can you help me?" I asked.

"From what you've told me, I can tell you a few things. First, the answer to your problem may be at the Deutschland Athletic Association. Second, your roommate Virgil was not who he pretended to be. Find out about him, where he came from. Third, it seems there is some truth to the money angle. See what you can learn about it."

He leaned forward again, elbows on the table. "Fourth," he said ominously. "If you're going to Deutschland, carry a gun." He reached under his sport coat, unholstered a snub-nosed twenty-two and slid it across the table toward me.

He smiled, flashing teeth as nicotine-stained as his yellowed fingernails.

"If you run into Von Schulte, shoot the bastard dead," he said. "God will forgive you."

I took the pistol and pocketed it. I'd been taken down twice in the last few hours, and I wasn't going to allow it to happen again. Anybody who planned any more violence against me was going to get paid back in kind.

Like the song says, "give peace a chance," right?

As I left the good father, I tossed a final glance at the picture of bad-ass Pig Pen McKernan, now nearly a month in his grave.

Hey, even the good die young.

***

I hadn't held a firearm since my tour in 'Nam. I killed men when I was over there but most of the time I couldn't say where, or when. I was in plenty of firefights but like the others around me I fired blindly, emptying clip after clip at the enemy, not knowing who or what I had hit. We knew we had scored by the body count after each fight. It was how the brass kept score. A high VC or NVA body count meant that we had won the battle. What we didn't know was the enemy was willing to sacrifice *all* his bodies to achieve victory, something we would never commit to.

So we won the battles but we lost the war.

Sacrificed thousands of boys for nothing and damned near toppled the government of the United States.

I did my tour and made it out alive, never really knowing how many I had killed in those faceless firefights.

But I came out one tough sonofabitch. Plinking rats in foxholes, I became an expert marksman, especially with a handgun, and could hold my own in a fist fight with anyone.

The pistol Abelard had given me was another matter. If I was going to shoot someone with it, it wouldn't be like 'Nam. I would have to look into his eyes and coldly pull the trigger.

Would I have the guts do it?

You bet your ass I would.

Picasso fought injustice with a paintbrush, and I would have preferred to do the same; but I doubt the men I was about to confront would be intimidated by my deft skills with oils and camel hair brush, my aggressive brush strokes or even my working class hero image.

This was definitely a case where the sword would be mightier than the pen (or in this case, brush).

It was 11 A. M. when I pulled up to the Deutschland Athletic Association. I knew that because Milwaukee's ubiquitous church bells were calling the faithful to worship and as an added bonus, striking out the time as well.

I decided against the front door, making my way instead around the back, where overflowing garbage cans lined both sides of a poorly-groomed alleyway. My feet crunched on broken glass as I crept up (like some b-movie World War Two spy) to a windowless metal slab that served as the back door to the Deutschland Athletic Association and tried the knob.

The door was open. Clutching the gun in my pocket, I stepped inside. The dank back hall reeked of sweat and echoed with the rumble of heavy weights being lifted.

I approached the gym from behind, threading my way through a musty locker room lined with rusted metal lockers and battered wooden benches. Somewhere beyond the locker room I heard a shower running and a throaty baritone mangling "Proud Mary." (An odd selection for a member of this particular organization. From what I had heard about them, "Deutschland Uber Alles" would have been more appropriate).

I pushed a door that opened to the gym. A tremendously-muscled man was standing on a plywood platform poised before the elephantine barbell. He chalked his hands, tightened the thick leather belt around his waist, slowly stepped to the bar, bent and grabbed it with a collar-to-collar grip. With a loud shriek he snatched the heavy weight overhead in one smooth motion, deftly and with great speed squatting under the barbell. Barbell balanced at arm's length, he smiled and dropped it from overhead, nimbly stepping back as it crashed down, sending earthquake-like tremors through the floorboards.

"Nice job," I said, walking up to him.

"Thanks," he replied, panting as if he'd just sprinted a quarter-mile. "State championships are coming up in two weeks. That was my opening weight for the snatch. Two-ninety-five. You think it looked easy?"

"Piece of cake."

He held out his hand. It was thickly callused and coated with white chalk. "Lenny," he said. He looked to be about my height and weight and sported a thick black mustache.

I took his hand and shook it. "Johnny."

"You got a good grip, Johnny. You work out?"

"I have a pair of fifty pound dumbbells in my apartment. I stay in shape with them."

"You should join the gym. We need lifters."

"Not today, thank you."

"Think about it. Now, what can I do for you?"

"I'm looking for Sol Katzenberg, Lenny."

He scratched himself with a finger, leaving a streak of white chalk on the tip of his nose. "You picked a strange playmate. Do you know the truth about Katzenberg?" he said.

"What 'truth?'"

"That Sol Katzenberg is actually Ernst Von Schulte, a Nazi and race-baiter."

"That should qualify him for membership here, shouldn't it?" I regretted the statement the minute it leapt from my mouth. I seemed to have gotten off on the right foot with Lenny and now I was jeopardizing our cordial relationship.

44

"Sorry," I said. "Pressure's getting to me, I guess."

The damage had been done, however. He pointed a finger and shook it in front of my nose. "You're a nosy guy, you know that?"

He was smiling, but the tone in his voice told me our brief honeymoon was over.

Tit for tat, I thought. I can be as shitty as he. "Actually, I'm a cabby. Sol Katzenberg or Ernst Von Schulte or whatever his name is, is holding a friend of mine against her will. The goddamned Nazi."

The smile fled from his face, replaced by a grim, thin-lipped frown. He ran his eyes over me like a man buying a slave at auction. I was waiting for him to ask me to open my mouth and flash my pearly whites so he could more closely check the merchandise.

"You a nigger?" he asked. The word jarred my sensibilities, as it always does. Every time I hear it I think of the good and gracious Grandma Jones, and try to reconcile its denigrating implications with that saintly woman. I never can.

But I kept my cool.

"Quadroon, actually. Whites won't accept me, and blacks don't want me," I replied, remembering the hostile Kareem and Mohammed at the Inasmuch Coffee House. From my perspective, prejudice cuts both ways, and just as deep.

He pointed to my Star of David. "And a Kike, too."

I remained unruffled.

"You're looking at the American melting pot in the flesh." My satiric wit was lost on him. He didn't chuckle, or even smile.

"The bastardization of the races. Mongrelization." He spoke in sharp, clipped sentences, spouting the party line. The same mantra as Abelard's Panthers, I noted.

"They say a mutt is smarter than a pure bred. How about you? You one hundred per cent Aryan?" I asked.

"All white, and proud of it."

"Like a bed sheet, maybe? With a pointed hood?"

Now he laughed.

"You don't scare easy. I like that. How about it, Axel? You think this nigger-hebe's a tough guy?"

I heard the creak of a floorboard behind me and turned quickly to meet the barrel of a .44 Smith and Wesson pressed against my cheek. Behind the gun was an enormous, pot-bellied biker in dirty bib overalls, a sleeveless leather vest with the word "Rumrunners" stenciled on the chest and a German

World War Two helmet with matching white swastikas painted on both sides balanced atop a grubby fat face.

I had a ballsy pal in 'Nam who always said that when in doubt, wing it with a smile. I crossed my arms over my chest in macho style and grinned; which was damned difficult, as the chill of the pistol barrel on my cheek reminded me of the seriousness of the situation.

"So how about it, Axel?" I said. "Is this nigger-hebe a tough guy?" I apologized *sotto voce* to the memory of Grandma Jones for using that damned word.

"Nah," replied Axel. His voice grated like a truckload of gravel being off-loaded onto the street.

"A smart-ass, maybe," he added. "But he's definitely no tough guy."

Abelard's gun lay impotent in my pocket. For all the good it would do me now, it might as well be lying on a tabletop in downtown Chicago, or on the moon.

"Says he's looking for Von Schulte, Axel. And a girl," Lenny looked at me. "What was her name?"

"Suzy Anger."

"Suzy Anger," he continued. "Can you help him?"

Axel made a little kissy-face at me.

"Love to," he said, motioning me to the back entrance by tickling my earlobe with the pistol barrel. It was then I noticed the woman leaning against the far wall in a studied pose. Long and lean, arms hanging loosely at her sides, a pencil-thin Virginia Slims cigarette ("You've come a long way, baby!") dangling from one corner of her mouth. She wore a gray, skin-tight, knee-length skirt and no-nonsense khaki cotton blouse. Her lush, shoulder-length honey blonde hair hung straight without the slightest hint of a curl.

Pinching the cigarette between an elegant finger and thumb, she took a long drag, exhaling the smoke with an overdramatic flourish. She dropped the cigarette on the gym floor, crushing it under a fashionable leather pump.

"Slow down, Axel," she said, pushing away from the wall, walking towards us. She moved fluidly, like a big cat confident of her place at the top of the food chain.

"H'lo, Miss Hart," he said, staring down at the toes of his hobnailed boots. The pugnacious Axel had suddenly gone soft.

Axel," she said, as she approached us. "Put the pistol down. I don't think we need to use brute force with a man as cultured as Mr. Jump."

As cultured as *Mr.* Jump? She obviously knew my name, but definitely not my character. It never crossed my mind to wonder how she was familiar with either. The way this crazy day was progressing, it was only normal to expect such things.

"Sure, Miss Hart. Whatever you say." Axel lowered the gun, a gesture I saw as something akin to the miracle of Our Lady of Fatima, or maybe Houdini's Water Torture act. Whoever this woman was who stood before me, she had the power to tame the savage beast, as evidenced by Axel's sudden change in attitude.

"We've met?" I asked her.

She wasn't a looker, but she had an aura about her; a powerful persona. She radiated an animal magnetism that both piqued my curiosity and excited me sexually. She held out a hand and I took it. Her fingers brought to mind Leonardo's magnificent Renaissance painting of Cecilia Gallerani; she of the long fingers stroking the ermine clutched to her tightly-laced bodice.

"We've never had the pleasure," she answered. Her handshake was warm, and firm; but something more was there: an elemental power. This was a woman used to giving orders, and having them obeyed.

"Johnny Jump," I said.

She released my hand. "Lenora Hart. I'm Suzy Anger's sister."

I thought, the Lord <u>does</u> move in mysterious ways!

***

"Suzy Anger's sister?" I asked.

"Not in the family sense," she answered. "We're sisters of the spirit, you might say. Childhood chums."

Then it dawned on me that I recognized the name. "<u>The</u> Lenora Hart?" I asked.

She nodded in what I perceived was smug assent. "The same," she said. *Vanitas vanitatum*, dear lady, I thought.

So this escapade could now boast of *two* faded 60s icons: Father Abelard and the lady who now stood before me.

In the early nineteen-sixties, Lenora Hart had emerged as the <u>enfant terrible</u> of the emerging feminist movement. A brilliant legal mind and skilled trial attorney, she had sued a number of big corporations on behalf of female employees and won nearly all of the verdicts, resulting in large cash settlements for her clients and binding agreements by the corporations that they would hire a prescribed number of female employees in executive positions. Her face had graced the cover of TIME magazine in nineteen-sixty-seven, and she had been both vilified and praised by prominent politicians, clergy and the talking heads on nightly network TV news. Her star had faded by nineteen-seventy, however, as others moved to the forefront of the feminist cause. She lost a half-dozen big cases as corporate America had gotten savvy to both her approach and her style, and were now better-prepared to do battle in the courtroom. It had been rumored that she had fallen hard, had hit the bottle and engaged in a series of ill-fated love affairs with rock stars and media types who had used and abused her, dumping her as they climbed the ladder of success. Then she had suddenly disappeared, gone missing, for the past two years. There were rumors that she had overdosed in a seedy motel room in Boise. That didn't seem to be the case, though. If this indeed was Lenora Hart. I conjured the image I remembered from the magazine cover. She indeed seemed to be one in the same with the photo. The longer I looked, the more I was convinced it was her.

"I thought you were dead," I said. "In Boise."

"Not hardly. And if I do exit this earth, it won't be in Boise. I'm very worried about Suzy."

"You'll excuse me, but I can't seem to put you and Suzy together. As 'sisters of the sprit,' I mean."

"No one ever could. I was the serious little girl, destined to be the hard-nosed professional. Suzie was Daddy's favorite. She was always regarded as the pretty one. Everyone always fawned over her. Even my own father."

There was bitterness in her voice, and I was about to tell her that she didn't rate so poorly in the looks department, to assuage her jealousy (if the way to a man's heart is through his stomach; then the way to a woman's is through her mirror), when she cut me off.

"What has happened to Suzie? Do you know where she is?"

I didn't buy her 'sisters of the spirit' spiel, so I wasn't about to divulge any information until I discovered what she was up to, and just how much she knew.

"The strong silent type, huh?" she said. "Well then allow me to be unsubtle. Did she mention anything to you about any money?"

"One million bucks, you mean?" I said, flaring in anger. "It's the cash your concerned about, not little 'sis of the spirit'?"

She took umbrage with the tone in my voice, set her jaw firmly as she spoke. "Please spare me your indignation, Johnny. Suzy is first and foremost in my thoughts, but I have spent the better part of the last two years searching for that money, and I don't intend on being snookered out of it."

Lenny, who had been silently watching our exchange, offered his observation.

"Everybody gets a slice of the cash, right?" he said. "You aren't gonna forget me and the boys, are you?"

"Yes, Leonard," she answered in a patronizing tone. "You and the boys will share."

"Why don't you let Axel do this guy, Lenora?" he said, jerking a thumb in my direction.

Axel brightened at the prospect of doing physical damage to yours truly. "I'll take him for a ride, Lenny," said Axel. "He'll talk. But quick.".

It was time to test Lenora Hart's control over them. "I think Miss Hart will object to your taking over, Lenny," I said, looking to her for approval.

"I'm afraid he's correct, Leonard," she said. "This is a delicate situation, and it will take finesse. You won't be able to bludgeon your way to a solution here. And it's *Miss* Hart, please. You don't know me well enough to call me by my first name."

I watched the brutish Lenny bristle at the put down and thought, God bless you, girl. If this was the army, they'd give you a medal.

"HOWEVER," she said with great emphasis. "If Mr. Jump won't cooperate, I'll expect you to utilize your special skills, Axel."

The biker grinned in anticipation of pounding your favorite cabbie into an unrecognizable pulp.

"I like the ride idea, however," she added. "My car's parked outside. Axel, you'll drive. I'll sit in back with Johnny, and we'll have a little talk."

"I should go, too," said Lenny. "Protect my investment."

"We'll have no need of you, Leonard. You just stay here and hold the fort. I'll see you later."

His biceps twitched involuntarily. "Oh, yeah? What happens if nigger-jewboy here spills his guts and you get the cash and scoot? What happens to me and the boys?"

"Never fear. You'll get your money. Like I said you would." End of discussion. She turned to Axel.

"Axel, get the car and bring it around back."

Axel shuffled away obediently. Lenora Barks gestured with an open hand, pointing the way out of the gym. "Let's go, Johnny."

Lenny stood on the lifting platform and watched us leave, coiled muscles quivering in anger.

Axel was parked in the alley, the automobile's busted muffler growling. Lenora Barks' wheels was a red and white nineteen-fifty-nine Chevy station wagon, rusted through at the rocker panels. A piece of cardboard box emblazoned with the words "Piggly Wiggly" was duck-taped over the missing left rear passenger window.

"Oh, how the mighty have fallen," I wisecracked.

"This to shall pass," she replied. "Once you tell me where the money is."

"I thought it was little sister you were worried about."

"Her, too. Now hop in."

She opened the rear passenger door and we slid inside.

Hands on the wheel, Axel said. "You should've taken Lenny, Miss Barks. If he thinks you're trying to fuck him, he'll come gunning for us. He's crazy."

"I believe I can handle him."

"Him, maybe, but what about the other twelve guys?"

"You let me worry about that, okay? Just drive. Take us out into the country. Maybe a bucolic setting will Johnny-jump-start his imagination." She said as she elbowed my ribs, giggling at the pun.

"Okay," growled Axel. "But I'm gonna keep an eye out for Lenny. He gets a case of the ass, we're all gonna die." He pulled out of the alley and into the street.

As if out of thin air, Lenora Hart produced a thirty-eight special and lightly tickled my cheek with the barrel. "Now, let's you and me have a nice long talk," she said. "And please tell me the truth. You're really a very beautiful man. I wouldn't want to have to shoot you."

Another creep with a pistol was threatening my life. I began to ask myself why I didn't go to the cops in the first place, and save myself all this trouble. But that had been an easy call. Back in my brief college days I 'dropped out,' and took a serious run at drugs, culminating in a freaked-out trip on purple haze which involved a terrified sorority girl, a gun and a midnight ride in a ripped-off convertible. I had been damned lucky to get a sympathetic judge, a veteran of Korea who, when he heard of my two purple hearts and silver star, gave me slap on the wrist: six months in the state lock-up at Green Bay. He understood that I had been re-living 'Nam that night. The car was an armored personnel carrier, the girl a VC captive, the stygian city streets a menacing jungle.

I kept my mouth shut while in prison, pumped iron, read the classics and vowed to pursue my art, no matter what the consequences. Apart from alcohol (which as you have seen I enjoy in abundance), I have never touched anything stronger than aspirin after that night.

With prison on my record I was reluctant to summon the constabulary, especially when we were talking murder, kidnapping, maybe rape and God knows what else. No matter whose fault; with my prison record I was tailor-made to take the fall. I would have to play this hand alone, minus the long arm of the law.

Axel maneuvered the Chevy through light traffic. I didn't know where we were going; but wherever it might be, I was sure it didn't bode well for me. Yet things weren't as bad as they'd seemed. Although Lenora Hart's pistol was nuzzling my cheek, I had options open to me.

For starters, I still had Abelard's pistol. It would have been easy to start blasting. Then the specter of my being an ex-con reared its ugly head. I imagined the scene: two dead in the car, me with the smoking gun.

Better, I thought, to wait and see how this would all shake out.

Above the roar of the car's muffler, I heard faraway church bells chiming the time.

Twelve strokes.

Noon.

How time flies when you're having fun.

PART FOUR
12:01 P.M. - 4 P.M.

Axel rolled down his window, and a shot of Arctic air rushed into the car.

"Dammit!" he cursed. "Goddamned snow on its way in April for Chrissakes! Won't be able to ride the hog at all in this weather!"

We were on a rustic country road west of Milwaukee, zipping past fallow fields dotted with farmer's homes with blistered white paint and bare-branched trees. Axel sang as John Kay and Steppenwolf howled "Born to be Wild" on the car's radio.

Lenora Hart had been prodding me with questions for the past half-hour and I had answered her honestly. I didn't know where the money was. Hell, I wasn't even sure there was any money. I'd been used and abused by an ever-increasing number of paranoid freaks who were convinced I held the secret to the whereabouts of a mythical million dollars, and I was getting pretty tired of it.

"What about your sister in spirit?" I asked her. "She may be laying somewhere, hurt. Or worse."

"Suzy can take care of herself. Just tell me where the money is," she sighed, exasperated.

"Where is it?" Axel said, never taking his eyes off the road. He'd been sucking off a bourbon bottle and chewing tobacco as he drove, and even from where I was sitting his breath reeked of Jim Beam and Red Man.

Lenora Hart brandished the gun. "I'll shoot you, if I have to." I knew it wasn't an idle threat.

"Where is *it*?" Axel asked again, raising his voice several decibels.

"Tell him, Johnny," Lenora said. "Tell *me* where it is."

I was positive she was going to shoot me, and soon, when suddenly Axel stared into the rearview and frowned. "Fuck!" he said, slamming a fist on the steering wheel. "Fuck, fuck, fuck!"

"What is it?" asked Lenora Hart.

"Here they come! I told you we should've taken care of Lenny!"

Jerking heads around, we peered out the rear window, spotting a snake-like string of Harley-Davidsons gaining ground on us, Lenny in the lead.

"Gun it!" commanded Lenora Hart.

Axel cursed. "This is all the speed I can get out of this heap. We should've taken him with or wasted him!"

"Water under the bridge. Lock and load," said Lenora. We'll have blow them off the highway."

I saw Lenny, guiding his bike with one hand, mad grin on his face, raise a pistol and fire. A sliver of flame streaked from the gun barrel and the station wagon's rear window shattered as the bullet struck the glass.

"Damn!" cursed Lenora, ducking. I huddled deep in the seat as she rolled down a window and returned fire, Axel hunched over the wheel like Mario Andretti at Indy.

"They're gonna kill all of us," he moaned. "That Lenny, he's one crazy motherfucker."

"Quit your whining and keep your eyes on the road, you goddamned crybaby!" she barked.

We raced down the two lane blacktop like stagecoach and Indians, guns blazing. *Where's law enforcement when you need them*, I thought. Right now, I would have given up my paints and brushes forever for one crummy cop, and never mind my prison record. Even that idiot FBI agent I had recently left to Sonny's tender mercies would have been a welcome sight.

I cautiously stuck my head up over the seat to see what in the hell was happening. Lenora Hart leaned out a window and fired. Hit squarely in the chest, one biker went down, skidding across the highway. A half-dozen of his compatriots smashed into him, flew like rag dolls and crash-landed, bouncing on the blacktop. No one could have survived the trauma. I was positive all of them were dead.

"Seven down!" she exulted as she reloaded.

As she spoke, a bullet screamed through the station wagon and plowed into Axel's neck. He jerked back then slumped forward, head striking the wheel. The out-of-control car began to fishtail, executing a series of donuts. It looped crazily for two hundred yards before it came to a sudden halt, stretched lengthwise across the highway, rocking on its wheels, threatening to tip.

The remaining half dozen Harleys careened toward the station wagon like heat-seeking missiles. I yanked the door open, grabbed Lenora Hart by the hand and leaped out of the car.

"Run!" I shouted as the bikes piled into the wagon one after the other. The car tipped, rupturing its gas tank and spilling petroleum and people across the road.

We raced through the drainage ditch at the side of the highway, up a small hill and down the other side as the car exploded, lifting up as if in slow motion, breaking in two in the center and then crashing onto the highway.

We hit the dirt behind the hill. A searing blast blew over our heads, carrying with it the screams of those being burned alive.

Curled in the safety of the womb-like earth, we waited until the cries of the dying were drowned by the crackling of flames.

A cacophony of sirens competed in the distance.

"*Now* comes the cavalry," I said, motioning toward an oak thicket a hundred yards to the east. "Let's get the hell out of here."

***

1-94 was less than two miles away. Like a charcoal sketch, a thick plume of smoke from the burning station wagon and motorcycles squiggled upward vertically, flattening itself against the storm clouds blanketing the sky. The chill in the wind and the pregnant thunderheads indicated we were in for a big blow, and soon. Probably rain, maybe snow.

We walked to a Milwaukee on-ramp and I stuck out a thumb. Shivering, Lenora Hart stared, doe-eyed, at me. Cute, I thought. She was playing a game, retreating into the guise of a damsel in distress. I played along as Sir Walter Raleigh.

"Cold?" I asked her, taking off my jacket and wrapping it around her.

"You don't have to do that if you don't want to," she said. "I threatened to shoot you just a few minutes ago."

"No sweat," I said. "I knew you wouldn't do it." This was fun. Point, counter-point, a game with no purpose.

"You run with a pretty dangerous crowd," I said.

"You'd be surprised at how many dangerous people I know, Johnny."

"No, I wouldn't."

She studied the smoke curling in the sky. "You know, I almost believe you. Maybe you don't know a damned thing about the money, do you?"

Thank God! Maybe I finally had gotten through to someone! Then again, we were only *playing* at sincerity.

"I would have shot you anyway, though."

"Maybe you would have, maybe you wouldn't have," I replied. "It's a moot point now."

"But now," she continued. "I don't want to. I may need you, what with Axel gone."

"Don't look to me to be your knight in shining armor, lady. I just want to find your 'sister in spirit,' see if she's okay."

She pouted her lips, contrite. "I have to confess, Johnny, that I lied. I'm only concerned abut the money."

I stared at the road before us. "Really," I sighed. Given the amount of lies I had been told and the number of lives expended in the past few hours because of those lies, it was no revelation. "I never believed you anyway."

She gave me a look that smacked of both appraisal and approval. "You're smart, aren't you? And brave, too."

"Smart, yes. But brave . . ." It was my turn to stare at the smoke in the sky. "I saw a lot of combat in Viet Nam, but I don't know if I've seen as much action as what's gone on today. And the way you handled yourself in the car back there. I'm impressed. That took a lot of balls."

"Maybe, but who cares? Balls alone won't cut it. It never has and it never will."

She reached into her pants pocket and took out a yellowed photo, handing it to me.

"I didn't want to show you this," she said. "But now I have no choice."

I studied the photo. A grainy black and white, it had yellowed with age, curled at its edges. In it a young man in a Nazi Waffen-SS uniform, hands on his hips, smiled broadly for the camera. Behind him three people hung from ropes on a thick tree branch. Their necks stretched obscenely like freshly-pulled taffy, their black tongues distended. One of them was a child, I would have bet no more than seven years old. Beyond them a broad plain stretched out in the distance, and beyond that a muscular column of smoke rose from what I assumed to be a burning village. It could have been eastern Poland, the Ukraine or Russia; probably the summer of 1942, when the Nazi death squads roamed the countryside of the conquered territories, liquidating Jews, Slavs and other "untermenschen"

A knot tightened in the pit of my stomach. I thought of my grandfather, of the war. "I've seen pictures like this before."

I attempted to hand the photo back, but she refused.

"Look at the Nazi," she instructed. "Study his face."

I did. It was a pleasant face, out of place in the gruesome setting. The smile should have belonged on a lineman who had just blocked a game-winning field goal, or a young man who recently bedded the high school prom queen.

Puzzled, I asked, "What should I be looking for?"

"You're an artist. Use your imagination. Put fifty pounds on him. Give him jowls and a beer belly, a moron's smile."

I did as she asked, sketching the features with my mind's eye.

I didn't want to admit to what I thought I saw.

It was Virgil as a young man.

She cracked a grim smile as the shock of recognition spread across my face.

"It's him, isn't it? Your roommate?"

"Lady, I believe in ghosts, UFOs and the story of Moses parting the Red Sea, but I don't know if I believe in *this*."

"You don't believe your own eyes? Or don't you want to?"

I stared again at the picture. It swam in and out of focus. First I was sure it was Virgil, then I wasn't. Then I was again.

"What in the hell are you trying to do to me? Where did you get this photo?"

She brushed the question aside with a wave of her hand. "That's inconsequential. What does matter is that you help me find the money."

"Ah. *The money*. What money? And who the hell is the real Virgil? Or do you know?"

"His real name is Hans-Dieter Dietrich. He was Waffen-SS, a high-ranking member of the execution squads that followed the Nazis into Poland, and then Russia. He managed to escape Europe disguised as a displaced person, aided by the Odessa and hefty payments in gold to corrupt Allied officials."

"How come I've never heard of him?"

"Do you know how many of these men--and women--there were? How many participated in the killings? How many never came to trial? How many faded into the woodwork, taking on new identities?"

"Thousands, probably."

"*Tens* of thousands. Your roommate's new persona was ingenious. A down-and-out drunk; a simple-minded buffoon who managed to shade an idealistic cabbie into letting him share an apartment rent-free."

I felt myself begin to tremble with rage. If it was true (and by the evidence of the photo she'd shown me, it might be) I had been duped on a grand scale.

Then again, she'd admitted to lying to me once. Why wouldn't she lie to me again?

Plus, I had a contrary story from Von Schulte that pegged Virgil as a pedophile and killer of three little black boys. However I sliced it (if I chose to believe either story), Virgil had been a very bad man.

I handed the photo back to her. "Right now, I don't know what to believe."

"Don't feel ashamed. How could you ever have known?"
She slipped the photo into my jacket pocket, stood on tiptoes and attempted to kiss me.

We were back at the game again, but this time I didn't want to play. It didn't take a rocket scientist to figure out that this was one cold, calculating lady, and that sex for her was only a tool to assist her in furthering her agenda.

I reluctantly pushed her away. She cocked her head, stared quizzically. "Don't you find me attractive?" she asked.

Sure I did, and I couldn't believe that I was passing up on what I knew would probably be a roaring good time. But it was Suzy Anger that had my heart, not Lenora Hart, even though she was at this moment very accessible.

Me, Johnny Jump. Man of the world. Cynic and arteest, prisoner of an uncontrollable passion. I admit Suzy had that effect on me; confident I'd wade naked through a river of fire for the benediction of her lips on mine.

"You didn't answer me," she said. Her mouth was very close to mine, and she smelled faintly of apple blossoms; probably one of those new "organic" scented shampoos.

I wanted to kiss her, but I was in a very complicated situation, and it would do no good to muck up the works. I left her question unanswered.

She shrugged off my rebuff. "It's your loss." It was obvious I had just made an enemy. A very dangerous one.

A car on the frontage road turned toward the ramp, and I hung out my thumb. A chubby woman in curlers gave us a perfunctory sidelong glance out of the passenger side window as the car sped past. Her lips were painted a garish red and she had applied clown-like rouge on her fat cheeks.

"So tell me Miss Hart, what should I believe?" I asked her, ducking a stone thrown by the passing auto's rear wheel.

"I said I lied, but there's some truth to everyone's story. Virgil didn't inherit the money, or embezzle it. He stole it from Polish and Russian Jews, and managed to smuggle it into this country. We know he has it hidden somewhere."

"And the tale Sol Katzenberg or Ernst Von Schulte or whatever his name told me, about the murdered boys in Illinois; that's a lie, too?" I quickly related the story.

"No. That is the truth. Dietrich was in Illinois. He was Potter's chauffeur. He did murder the boys. It's what tipped us off to where he was.

"Diedrich's 'specialty' as a Waffen-SS was the murder and genital mutilation of children," she continued. "Young boys, specifically. The Potter case made international headlines. It was a simple matter of putting two and two together. He was our man, we were sure of that."

She was painting a picture of my friend that I had could hardly believe, that I struggled to comprehend.

"Von Schulte said Suzy was Virgil's daughter."

Her face corkscrewed in intense hatred. "That man would do anything, say anything to protect himself from us."

"So you say. You keep referring to 'us,' and 'we.' Who are you?"

"Me? I'm a Jew and an exterminator, Johnny Jump. I rid the world of vermin."

"A Jew?" I said skeptically. I couldn't remember that being part of her bio when she was rich and famous. I told her so.

"No one knew back then. I was ashamed of my heritage, as were my parents. We lived a comfortable life as Gentiles in a Gentile world. I only recently reconciled myself to my faith"

Taking into account my family's history, I could empathize with her argument. "What did you mean by calling yourself an 'exterminator?'" I asked.

"I'm a Nazi hunter. I bring murderers to justice."

"Like Simon Wiesenthal?"

"No. Mr. Wiesenthal brings the infamous to trial. I belong to a shadow organization who has already tried and
passed judgment on those we seek. We only need to find them to carry out sentence."

"Then your people killed Virgil?"

She laughed mirthlessly. "Not hardly. We are Old Testament folks. 'Do unto others as they have done to the world' is our motto. A bullet through the heart was poor

retribution for the horrible crimes Dietrich visited on innocent children."

"Who shot my roommate then?"

"Nazis, Johnny. People who knew him. People he trusted."

"Why?"

"Because we had found him, and they feared he would lead us to them. Through him we had already found Von Schulte, posing as a Jew running a bookstore. We would have discovered--and carried sentences out-- against dozens more. Plus, we wanted that money. It would have helped fund our organization for years to come."

"So where's this million dollars?"

Her eyes searched mine. "I was hoping you could help us find it, Johnny." Sweet Jesus, she was back at it again!

A second car approached and stopped when I extended my thumb. A long hair at the wheel rolled down the window. The pungent odor of marijuana fumes wafted past my nose.

He brushed stringy blonde hair out of his eyes and stared vacantly at me. "Where to, man?"

"Milwaukee," I said, relating my cab's whereabouts.

"Hey, we'll take you right to your front door, huh Rudy?" he said to his companion, an identical long hair in flannel shirt and bell bottom jeans peppered with a rainbow of multi-colored patches.

"Cool," said Rudy. The Grateful Dead's "Sugar Magnolia" blasted on the car radio, and he kept time by slapping the dash like it was a pair of bongos.

We climbed inside. I wanted to get back to my cab and then to my apartment and put this day behind me.

She must have read my thoughts.

"Don't think you can walk away, Johnny," she said. "They won't let you. *I* won't let you."

Now it was my eyes that searched hers, looking for a sign that she was indeed telling the truth.

Pablo could be a real shit to his women. I couldn't. You look into a face like Lenora Hart's and sometimes you want to, *need* to, believe them. Dive head-first off a towering cliff into unknown waters.

But I wasn't going to leap to any life-threatening conclusions.

Not just yet, anyway

PART FIVE:
4:01 P.M. - 8 P.M.

Rudy puckered his lips as he sucked a giant hit off a smoldering joint and handed it back to me.

"Jamaican, man," he said as he exhaled. "The best."

I waved off the joint. I've already explained my stand on drugs. In another life, I blew dope in 'Nam, but just to take the edge off between patrols. When the action got hot and heavy, I wanted a clear head. Staying alive had been my primary purpose there. I felt the same urge for self-preservation in my current situation.

"That's cool, man," he said. He took another hit and passed the joint to the driver, who coughed as he inhaled. Rudy began banging on the dash again, this time to the Jefferson Airplane's "White Rabbit."

As we barreled down the highway, I dissected the wild stories and hair-raising events of the last few hours, and the only common thread I could see was money. Whatever the truth was and whoever was to be believed, the money was always there: one million dollars in cold cash, waiting for the man or woman lucky enough or brutal enough to wrest it away from the others.

I was convinced that Virgil was more than a harmless old vagrant. For evidence, I thought back to a few weeks ago.

I'd been drinking pretty heavy that night, first at a string of local shot-and-beer joints then later at home with Virgil. The bleary-eyed old drunk had downed the better part of a six-pack and was beginning to get maudlin.

"You know, Johnny, you been so good t'me," he said, flashing lachrymose peepers, (It was his standard line when he got drunk, which was often; and it embarrassed me) as he sipped his sixth beer.

"It's nothing, Virgil," I insisted. (My standard reply).

A string of spittle leaked from the left side of his mouth, trickled down his jowl and dangled like a teardrop off his chin.

"I done things in this life, Johnny. Bad things."

"We all have, pardner."

"No," he'd said. "I done <u>bad</u> things, things I gotta pay for."

"You're no different than anyone else, Virgil. We'll all have to answer for our sins some day."

"Johnny, I get so scared sometime." He shivered, bunched up his shoulders as if a serpent had curled around his neck. "They're all dead, and they're gonna get me some day."

"What are you talking about, buddy?"

"Ghosts, Johnny."

"There's no such things as ghosts, Virgil." I do believe in ghosts, but I didn't see the sense in telling him that. Not at that particular point in time, anyway.

"But Johnny, there is. I see 'em every night. In my dreams."

Then he began to cry. An eerie, muffled wail.

I had marked it down to a mild case of delirium tremens, which for a man with Virgil's alcoholic inclinations would not have been unusual.

But thinking back to Lenora Hart's tale of marauding Nazis and Katzenberg's horrendous story of pedophilia and murder, the seemingly innocuous conversation took on a terrible, crystalline truth.

There was obviously more than met the eye to my roommate - something dark and sinister.

I knew that before the day was over, I would know the truth, and it terrified me.

Back at the Deutschland Athletic Association, I pointed out my cab to the hippies.

"You're sure you don't want something for the ride?" I asked them as I climbed out of the car. "A couple bucks, maybe?"

"Nah," said the driver. "Just stay cool, pardner. Peace, love and rock and roll."

"What's your name, in case we meet again? So I can return the favor."

He flashed a smile. "Me, man? I'm the Lone Ranger. Rudy here is Tonto."

Rudy grinned and nodded. "Cool," he said, banging on the dash, keeping time to Grand Funk's "I'm Your Captain."

"Everybody," he crooned in a raspy voice. "Listen to me, and return me my ship . . ."

We stood curbside as they pulled out into the street. I could hear a muffled tremolo as they headed off to points unknown, adrift in a fog of marijuana fumes and psychedelic incandescence.

"I'm your captain, yeah yeah yeah yeah . . ."

***

Lenora Hart broke the silence.

"You're having a difficult time aren't you?" she said. She dug the photograph out of my pocket and jabbed a finger at it. "Believing that the man in that picture could be the same man who lived with you for two years."

"Yes." I found myself morbidly drawn to the photo, especially to the child hanging from the tree limb. His eyes bulged, and his face had a waxy, doll-like sheen. It disturbed me greatly, yet I couldn't take my eyes off it.

She read my emotions. "They were Jews, Johnny. Like your grandfather. Innocent people. Innocent women and children."

"It's . . . too much to comprehend," I replied as I attempted to reconcile the image of the brutal SS officer in the photo with that of the harmless old man who shared my apartment.

"Johnny, if you know anything about the money please tell me. It will be used to avenge those murdered children."

"I've been told so many stories in the past few hours. Who in the hell do I believe? What do I believe?"

She touched me lightly on the cheek. "Poor Johnny."

I took her hand away. "No pity, please."

We were ensconced at the lunch counter in one of my favorite haunts when I was a Brady Street resident: the Oriental Drugs on Farwell and North. Adjacent to the equally eclectic Oriental Theater, the drug store was rendezvous point for hard hats, long hairs, working folks and oddballs. It was a popular stop for east siders, and offered typical lunch counter fare. I had ordered a cup of coffee and a BLT, Lenora a hot chocolate and tuna salad on whole wheat.

I absently stirred my coffee with a spoon. Outside, a light dusting of snow began to fall. Parked at the curb, my cab appeared ghostlike, as if it were wrapped in a diaphanous shroud.

Ghosts again. I had spooks on the brain. Somewhere, someone's spirit cried out for vengeance. Somebody Virgil had wronged. I felt it deep in my heart.

The unwanted spring snowfall created an atmosphere of silent melancholy among the restaurant's customers. A few coughed. One scratched his cheek with the tines of his fork. Watching the snowfall, a woman cursed between mouthfuls of soup.

"Damned winter won't ever let go," said a man at the counter with fat lips and thick nose hairs.

"Easter's only a few days away," chorused a plump lady whose rotund ass threatened to burst her polyester slacks as she plunked onto a counter stool.

"We're supposed to get two feet of the white stuff by tonight," said the waitress behind the counter, sticking a number four pencil in her beehive hairdo as she set a cup of coffee and a donut in front of a customer.

I observed them as if they were a Shakespearean drama and I an offstage spirit, unable to be seen or heard.

Lenora tapped my shoulder. "So what are you going to do, Johnny?"

"Go home. Sleep it off. Maybe this is all a twisted nightmare. One too many boilermakers."

"It's not. And you can't go home. Or hide. They'll find you; and when they do, they'll hurt you."

"'They' again."

"Von Schulte. The Nazis."

"Why would they hurt me? I took their pal in. Gave him three hots and a cot."

"The money, Johnny. They want the money. They think you know where it is."

She stroked the back of my hand with hers. I felt myself go soft, like a kitten, and I wanted to purr.

"Think back, Johnny. Did he tell you anything that might lead to the money?"

I pulled my hand away and shoved it in my pocket. It cuddled against Abelard's twenty-two.

"It's always the money, isn't it?" I said. "What do you *really* want?"

"The money, Johnny, and that's the truth."

"A million dollars buys a lot of truths, Miss Hart."

She ignored the insult. "Think back, Johnny. Maybe he told you where the money was, without you realizing it."

I did recall a night when Virgil said "I'm gonna pay you back some day. I got money, you'll see."

What did that mean? They were the hallucinations of a man gone to seed on hard living and liquor, as I saw it; and if he were alluding to a great fortune, where was the clue to its whereabouts in his statement?

"I need a little time," I said.

"I need to use the bathroom," she replied, rising from her stool. "I'll be back in a few minutes." Every set of male eyes in the joint followed her as she walked to the ladies' room; feline in heat, on the prowl .

"More coffee?" asked the waitress, filling my cup when I nodded in the affirmative.

As I sipped the weak brew, lost in thought, two men took the stools on either side of me, wedging against me tightly like bookends.

I recognized them and groaned.

Hakeem and Mohammed in black shades and black tams stared impassively at the plate glass window and the falling snow outside.

Mohammed spoke first, out of the side of his mouth. "Father wants to see you. Now."

"And what if I don't want to go?"

"Then we'll have to make you," said Hakeem.

I pulled out the twenty-two and jammed it in his gut.

"I don't think you can."

Mohammed reached into his coat and slowly lifted a Colt .44 magnum six shooter with a four inch barrel out of its shoulder holster and stuck it in my ribs. At that precise moment, a waitress at the far end of the counter spilled hot coffee on a customer's lap. The man howled and jumped up, the waitress screamed and everybody's attention was directed to the noisy scene while our life-and-death drama unfolded unnoticed, as if the three of us were invisible.

Mohammed leaned over and placed his lips against my ear. His fetid breath was damp and sticky.

"Now here's the scenario," he whispered. "You're going to pop Hakeem with your little gun, poke a teeny hole in his tummy and he's going to leave here on his own two feet with a bellyache. Then I'm going to blow a hole in your chest," (He jammed the .44 deeper into my ribcage for emphasis) "And you are going to exit this fine establishment in a body bag."

He pulled back and asked in a normal voice, "Is that the way you want it, Johnny Jump?"

It was impossible to argue with his flawless logic. I put the twenty-two back into my pocket.

"I'm waiting for a lady," I said. "She's in the bathroom."

Mohammed removed the gun from my ribs and slid it back into the shoulder holster. The spilled coffee incident had ended, and everyone quietly returned to their business.

"Cherchez la femme, half-ass. She'll keep," he said.

I tossed a five spot on the counter to cover our food and drinks.

"You're leading the way," I said.

They guided me out of the drug store, Mohammed in front, Hakeem following behind.

The bumblebee-yellow Dodge Super Bee that had tailed me on my way to Milwaukee pulled to the curb across the street from the drug store as I followed Hakeem and Mohammed to their car. The same shadowy figure sat at the wheel, unrecognizable behind the light curtain of snow. If he'd been following me all the while, he'd done a damned good job of it. I hadn't seen him, or his conspicuous car.

As I watched the Dodge I cursed myself for a fool. Everybody, it seems, knew where I was going but me.

I'd not only lost control of the situation, I'd lost both Suzy Anger and Lenora Hart.

And Abelard's twenty-two proved to be useless against the nut cases I'd bumped heads with in the last few hours.

***

After I related what had transpired at the Deutschland Athletic Association, and the shoot-out on the highway, Father Abelard said, "They wanted to rough you up, huh?"

"Sure as shooting, father. When you're a white supremacist Nazi biker, a combination nigger-jewboy like me is quite a plum. Sort of like a flesh and bone piñata."

He laughed grimly. "You've got a sense of humor. That's good. I'm sorry that happened. I didn't intend for it to go that way."

"*You* didn't intend for it?"

"I let them know you were coming."

"You knew what was going to happen?"

"I thought they'd tip their hand, and they did."

"Tip their hand?"

"They were after more than just Jew-baiting, Johnny."

"I know that. They were after a mythical million dollars."

"Not so mythical," he replied.

He held a lit match to the end of a fresh cigarette and took a deep drag. He blew the smoke out slowly, fishing out a fleck of loose tobacco stuck between his teeth with the tip of his finger.

"We're at war, Johnny Jump. You of all people should know that, being both black and Jewish."

"Father, I'm a portrait artist, an admirer of Picasso, a cabby and a hard drinker. Apolitical and proud of it."

"You can't avoid the issues in these politically charged times, Johnny."

Hakeem reached between us with the coffee pot and refilled our cups. He removed the shades. His eyes burned with contempt as he stared at me. I didn't buy Abelard's explanation that some people hate for no particular reason. There was more to it than that. I put the question to them.

"What's your problem with me?" I asked.

"I'll tell you," replied Mohammed. "You said your grandma was black?"

"Yes. So what?"

"Means she was raped by a white man. You're the product of a sexual assault, half-ass."

"It's *quarter-ass*, pal. And my Grandmother wasn't raped, she married my grandfather. Out of love and respect."

"No black woman would willingly go with a white man. Your granny was violated," said Mohammed.

"Listen, numb-nuts," I said. "You *ever* bring up my grandmother in conversation again, I'll kill you."

"Anytime, baby," Hakeem hissed in reply.

I turned my attention to the priest. "I'll tell you what, father," I said. "I have never been made more unpleasantly aware of my racial and religious heritage than when I'm around 'enlightened' folks like you and the rest of the 'revolutionary' crowd. In my social circles, people take me for what I am. No more, no less. But you people who pretend to be color-blind strike me as being the worst bigots. You're ashamed of yourselves, and you try to pass that shame on to others."

He lay his cigarette down on the table and clapped slowly. "Bravo. Fabulous speech. But it won't reverse history. We're on a fast train to dynamic change, and no one can stop it."

For that brief moment, I glimpsed the fire in the belly that had once been Father Abelard's trademark. I understood how he had shaken up not only Milwaukee, but the Church and the nation as well.

I also knew his cause offered lock-step dogma in place of what it wanted to destroy. As shitty as these 'revolutionaries' felt it was, I pretty much liked the world. With a few glaring exceptions, it was basically a free and easy place, where the unshackled spirit could soar.

"Those bikers charcoaled on the highway were *your* pals, weren't they?" I asked.

"I work with many organizations, to advance the cause.

"The end justifies the means?"

"Something like that, but it's past history."

He leaned forward, elbows on the table. "So how about it, Johnny Jump. Will you join us to create a better world?"

I felt that Abelard would soon be spouting the virtues of Chairman Mao, waving his little red book. I had seen the end results of that little red book in the jungles of Viet Nam: a family of seven spread-eagled on the ground, bellies opened with axes, privates dug out with butcher's knives. I don't condone what we're doing there; but I'll be goddamned if I'm going to have an uninformed goody-two-shoes tell me what band of murderers I'm going to join forces with.

That choice will always remain with me.

"Suzy Anger," I said. "I want her here with me. Now."

I jerked a thumb at Hakeem and Mohammed, waiting patiently in a far corner.

"Send Pete and Repeat to bring her here."

"An unfortunate choice of words, half-ass" said Mohammed, clucking his tongue as Hakeem did a slow burn. "I'm afraid my brother has taken offense."

Hakeem made a menacing step towards me, but the priest waved him off. He obeyed, but reluctantly.

"We don't need this shit, father," said Mohammed.

The priest raised an open hand in a conciliatory gesture. "Later, Mohammed," he said.

He turned to me. "You've got a death wish, don't you?"

"No," I replied, raising my voice. "But I know I'm through taking shit. Yours and everybody else's. I want Suzy Anger brought to me."

"Tread softly around that lady, Johnny," said the priest. "Just what do you know about her?"

"Everything. Nothing."

"Aptly put. No one, it seems, knows much about Ms. Anger."

He used the new prefix 'Ms.,' and the sound of it rang funny in my ears.

"How about you? You seem to be bosom buddies."

"Suzy and I are merely acquaintances. Two ships that passed in the night."

"Lenora Hart?"

He made a big show of nonchalantly tracing a figure eight with his finger over the table top. "Oh, my," he said. "Now she's popped up, too? The proverbial fly in the ointment.""

"In the flesh. And she wants the million."

He chuckled. "You know, she defended me once. I and a group of others invaded a selective service office and destroyed their records. She got us off on a technicality, and in her summation, gave a withering denunciation of the war in Viet Nam. She was magnificent."

"I remember it well. It was a big deal. Back then."

He shook his head slowly. "It's sad to see formerly principled woman involved in this sordid money grab."

"Men of God, too," I replied. "What makes you any different than her?"

"I can't explain it except to say that the Lord moves in mysterious ways, Johnny," he answered, dodging the question. "How did you manage to extricate yourselves from that highway firefight?"

"Blind luck and some good shooting. A man in your profession might have called it divine intervention."

He stroked his chin thoughtfully. "You may be correct on that account. We're on the right side of this fight."

"'*We?*'"

"Yes, we. You've been drafted, Johnny, to assist in the greatest battle of this century. America is in revolt, and the old order is going down in flames. Out of those flames a new, more just society will rise; like a phoenix out of the ashes."

The argument, which a few short years ago seemed to have so much meaning, now rang hollow. It was disturbing, how he could shift gears so quickly and lapse into sociological claptrap. Abelard, it seemed, was a shaman of lost causes.

"Bullshit, father. You can walk that walk and talk that talk, but all your over-heated rhetoric won't change a goddamned thing."

I reached across the table and tapped the back of his hand with my finger. "It all boils down to money, father. The dough-re-mi. This is a grab for cash, pure and simple; and all the glorified speeches in the world won't whitewash that fact."

"Magnificent words. You should consider a career in politics."

"Not me. Politicians are basically unhappy people. That's why they pander for votes. They want love and acceptance, the reassurance of the limelight."

"So you're that most rare of individuals, a happy man?"

"Until today I was the happiest man in the world. I drove a cab. I drank. I painted on weekends. I had a part-
time girlfriend who likes me a lot, maybe loves me a little. I paid my rent on time and had enough left over to eat when I was hungry and drink when I was dry."

"You make it all sound so simple."

"It *is* that simple."

"Then I'll give you it straight. The whole story."

He sat ramrod stiff in the old wooden chair, took a hit off his cigarette and set it down, watching impassively as it burned a hole in the table.

"In nineteen-fifty-two, a gang of thugs robbed a suburban Chicago bank. They weren't your run-of-the-mill stick-up artists. They had a carefully constructed plan, meticulously detailed. In and out, grab the cash. A lot of cash, by the way. The bank was in a well-heeled suburb and they hit it on a Friday morning, when the vault was loaded with cash for paychecks, plus other things."

He paused, picked up the cigarette, took a slow drag and crushed the burning butt between thumb and forefinger. It was a cheap display of imperviousness to pain, and I wasn't impressed.

"Everything went as planned," Father Abelard continued, dropping the cigarette to the floor. "Until they got into the getaway car. Three of them had robbed the bank, a fourth waited in the car. When the three jumped in the auto with two duffel bags loaded with money, the driver calmly pulled a gun and shot each in the head. Then he took the sacks and *walked* away, disappearing around a street corner. Just like that, he was gone with over a million dollars in cash. The police arrived a few minutes later and gave chase, but it was like he'd strolled through a wall into another time zone, leaving three dead partners as mute witnesses to the crime. There were no prints on the car, no clues whatsoever. The car itself had been stolen, and there were no eyewitnesses who could give a clear description of the driver."

He held his hands out, palms up like a supplicant at Mass. "Bingo. The perfect crime."

"Thrilling story, father. Something right out of *The Twilight Zone*. But what does it have to do with anything?"

"The getaway driver was your roommate, Virgil."

I laughed. "First a pedophile and murderer, then a vicious Nazi, now a bank robber? Next you'll be blaming Virgil for the Crucifixion."

"*Think*, Johnny Jump. If you had found a man you had searched for all your life, and he had something you desperately wanted, something you knew that he would never reveal the location of, how would you get to him?"

He answered his own question. "Through his friends, Johnny. And old Virgil had but one friend on this earth--you, a loyal true-blue stand-up kind of guy."

We were eye to eye, and nobody blinked.

"You still don't get it, do you?" he said. "You get through to a stand-up, loyal, true-blue friend by creating wild stories about his roommate, stories that would make him turn on his pal in a heartbeat. Create a bogeyman."

Now I blinked.

"And if his pal is part-Jew, with a black grandmother, and a grandfather who survived the Holocaust, what better bogeyman than a Nazi, a defiler of little black boys?"

"*Then* spin the tale of murdered Jews and Nazis and buried treasure?" I said.

"Exactly."

I leaned back, hands folded in my lap. "I'm disappointed, father. Your story is insipid. Absolute b.s."

"Suzy got to you, didn't she?"

I bristled. "Not hardly."

"You're blinded by love, and I don't blame you. She has that effect on people." The wistfulness in his voice sounded like he had bedded Suzy himself. I had a disturbing vision of her raising the skirts of his cassock, spidery fingers probing underneath, fondling him.

I pointed an accusatory finger. "You're asking me to refute her story, and believe yours. One is more fantastic than the other."

"Except I'm telling the truth."

"*You* sent me to the Deutschland Athletic Association, where I was kidnapped by Lenora Hart."

"If you remember correctly, Suzy guided you to me, and I sent you to Deutschland. Her idea, not mine. Lenora was unexpected; an unwelcome surprise."

"You're saying it was a set-up?"

"It was *supposed* to be, but it got out of hand. We never thought there would be any bloodshed, but there were major miscalculations. When you ally yourself with psychotics like those bikers or Lenora Hart, you're taking your chances. Look at the Stones at Altamont, with the Hell's Angels. This was basically the same thing." He shook his head slowly, feigning sorrow. "Stupid," he mumbled. "Stupid."

"So I've been hosed from start to finish?"

"It was a show put on for your benefit, in hopes you'd reveal the location of the million dollars. All engineered by Ms. Anger."

"I don't know where any money is. I don't even know if there is any money! When will you people get that through your thick heads?"

"Are you absolutely sure of that?" he asked, his voice thick with skepticism.

I slammed a fist on the table. "Yes!"

He stared at me clinically, as if I were a bug pinned to a board. "Don't be angry with yourself, Johnny," he said. "You fell for it hook, line and sinker. But with the beautiful Ms. Anger spinning the web, who could resist?"

"So there are no Nazis. No killer of the Potter children?" I took out the photo that Lenora had given me and laid it on the table. "What about this?"

He stared grimly at the snapshot. "By the time you were showed this gruesome picture, you were willing to believe anything anyone told you. You see, Suzy created an elaborate *roman a clef* to dupe you into revealing the location of the million dollars."

"But this *is* Virgil!" The words rang hollow. I had become Suzy's surrogate in her absence.

"If you *want* to believe in advance it is he, then certainly you could make the leap in logic. But it isn't."

"So who is Ernst Von Schulte?"

"Suzy Anger's lover."

I felt my spine macerate as I settled deeper into my chair.

"The oldest game in the book" said the priest. "*La Belle Dam Sans Merci.*" He intoned lines from the poem.

> *"I saw pale Kings, and Princes too,*
> *"Pale warriors, death pale were they all;*

I completed the stanza:

> *"They cried 'La belle dam sans merci*
> *Hath thee in thrall!'"*

"I know the poem, father. And I don't see a correlation between Suzy Anger and John Keats. Or me, for that matter."

He regarded me with curiosity. "You're a strange sort of cabby, quoting Keats. Do you still have my gun?"

"Yes. But it doesn't seem to scare anyone very much."

"With a gun like that, you don't try to scare people. You shoot them. Up close, and quickly."

"What?" I asked incredulously.

"You could settle the score. Today."

"What kind of Christian are you, Father Abelard?"

"The pragmatic kind. A Christian who realizes that to make an omelet, a few eggs have to be broken."

"Lenin said that, not Jesus."

"Yes, and he was correct."

"What's in this for you? The money?"

"A million dollars buys a lot of political power. We could change the world."

Another about face. From Lenin to Crosby, Stills and Nash.

"Virgil is dead," I replied. "His secret died with him."

"But he's not dead."

"I saw him. Sprawled out on my floor. Shot dead."

"Oh, they shot him, all right. He wouldn't surrender his secret, not even under the threat of death, so they had to turn to you. Think, Johnny. Back to what transpired in your apartment. Didn't Suzy make a pass as you knelt to inspect the body? She was preventing you from taking a closer look, seeing that Virgil was merely wounded. They needed to have you believe he was dead. They have him holed up somewhere back in your hometown. When you tell them what they want to know, they'll kill him."

"But he never told me anything."

His eyes patronized mine, and with good reason. I felt like the world's biggest horse's ass. A pawn moved hither and yon at the whim of a malevolent and unstable hand. It was time to back out. Cut my losses and run.

"No more," I said. "I'm through."

"You can't say that, Johnny. There's no way out, except to finish them off before they decide you're really telling the truth about not knowing where the money is. Then your life is forfeit."

"How did they find Virgil?"

"She found him. It took her twenty years, but she had the motivation. You see, one of those three men Virgil shot in the getaway car was her father."

"Another revelation! When are you going to get to the part about the alien abductions?"

"This is no joke. There's more than the money for her in this," he said. "She wants revenge, too. Which makes her all the more dangerous."

"Suzy," I muttered, clenching my fists.

"I can imagine your distress, Johnny. I know where Suzy is. Mohammed will show the way. Once there, you can do what you feel you have to do."

The room was spinning as I tried to digest the truths, half-truths and outright lies I'd been told in the past few hours. I felt an ominous presence behind me and turned to see stone-faced Mohammed, directly behind my chair.

"Let's go, man," he said. He grabbed my shoulder as he pulled my chair out with me still on it.

I stood and slapped his hand away. "Get your fucking hands off me!"

"Mohammed!" Abelard barked at him like a man at a vicious Doberman he wasn't sure he could control.

The black man backed off. "Someday, baby," he said to me. "You and me. One on one."

"Any time," I said. "Any place."

"Enough!' commanded Abelard. Mohammed and I stood in stony silence, eyeing each other like two heavyweights in the center of the ring as the ref recited the final instructions.

"One last thing, Johnny," said the priest. "If they feel you're holding out on them they'll strike out at someone close to you."

"My mother and grandmother are dead. My father's gone. Who else is there?"

"That part-time girlfriend you talked about," he continued. "What did you say her name was? Jennifer?"

I *hadn't* told him her name.

Now they were dragging Jennifer in on this, too.

"I'll kill the man who touches her." The statement sounded silly the second it escaped my lips. Captain America, me.

"She'll still be just as dead," said Abelard.

I left with Mohammed, wondering who was telling the truth. But at this point, who the hell cared?

With Jennifer suddenly threatened, there was nothing left to do but finish the game.

***

The driving snow was beginning to pile up on the streets. Soon the storm would carry with it the full force of the northeasterly gales that swept down from Canada across the flat, frigid expanse of lakes Superior and Michigan. A freak spring storm was not unusual for the area. I had seen them plow down on us in early May, knocking buds off fruit trees and killing spring flowers.

But they still depressed the populace, and deflated the optimism of spring.

I often wondered if Pablo had been raised in a cold climate, how his art would have been affected. Personally, I feel he'd never have gotten out of his blue period.

No one who is raised in a climate that delivers twenty degrees below zero temperatures in the winter and one hundred degrees plus in the summer can be unaffected.

It's why we in the Chicago-Milwaukee corridor have produced so many writers, poets and actors.

But not so many painters.

Had he been born and raised here, I believe Picasso would have become a thespian. He has an affinity for the stage, and is quite the ham. Someone who enjoys creating myths and then spending a lifetime conjuring those myths into reality, performing them for public adulation.

Like Suzy Anger.

If I was to believe Father Abelard, she had Academy Award abilities. Best Actress in the Life-and-Death category.

I didn't need to hang around to experience any more of her star qualities. I could have driven off to home and comfort and a case of beer, bottle of bourbon, my paints and Jennifer in my warm bed.

Then again, Abelard had said Jennifer was in danger. From the same people who had casually shot old Virgil, leaving him stretched out on my apartment floor like that freshly-slaughtered horse.

Father Abelard also had stated that Virgil was alive. If it was true, I wanted to find him.

I also wanted to discover just who in the hell was telling the truth; and what the truth really was.

And how about the money? One million dollars that everybody was convinced I knew the whereabouts of?

That was the least of my concerns. Money, lots of it, carries great responsibility. If the tale of lost loot was true, and I found it, I didn't know if I wanted to shoulder that burden.

I felt thankful that at least it was Sunday, and that the traffic was light on Milwaukee's city streets as I drove to the rendezvous point given to me by Mohammed, a decaying movie palace just west of the Milwaukee River on Wisconsin Avenue.

I dropped Mohammed off at the corner of Sixth and Wisconsin, in front of a Marc's Big Boy restaurant. He leaned through my open window.

"Enjoy th' flick," he chuckled. "And keep your gun handy. That lady friend of yours is no one t' mess with. She gives you any trouble, shoot the bitch." Same instructions as his mentor, Abelard, had given me.

He became somber, stone-faced. "I want you to stay alive, Johnny Jump. I want you for myself."

For once I shelved the repartee. If he wanted a piece of me, that was fine. I'd accommodate him later. I pulled away from the curb as he strutted cockily into the restaurant.

I parked the cab in a downtown lot a block from the theater and hustled my way through the driving snow to the movie house. The yellow Dodge Super Bee was parked in front. My tail was here. Maybe with Suzy Anger, or maybe just following her as well. Whatever the reason, I was finally going to get the chance to meet him. I rubbed snow off a window and peered inside the Dodge. The car was empty, spic-and-span, void of any clues that might point to the identity of the mysterious driver.

There was a thin line of pickets outside the theater, carrying signs that read "This theater insensitive to Italian-Americans." I crossed the picket line (a couple of the protestors shook angry fists at my nose, but I blew them off), wondering what in the hell the protest was about, purchased a ticket and went inside, shaking snow off my jacket.

I bought a box of popcorn and a Coke at the concession stand. I hadn't had anything to eat since the sugar cookie I had purchased at the bakery earlier in the morning. My stomach growled, demanding to be placated.

Clutching popcorn and soda, I opened the door to the darkened theater and slipped inside, standing at the back and scoping the sparse audience to see if I could make out Suzy Anger's location.

The movie was "The Godfather," which recently won three Academy Awards. Which ones, I don't know and don't much care. I don't like movies, their artifice. Or television, either. I went seven years without a TV until Jennifer complained and I bought a second-hand black-and-white screen from TV Tommy's Second Hand Shop and set it up in my apartment. When Jennifer is spending the night she enjoys watching the campy horror show hosted by "Svengoolie" on WFLD Channel Thirty-Two out of Chicago. Virgil will sometimes join her, and the two howl in delight at the show's outrageous antics.

I usually sit in the kitchen, door shut to muffle their laughter, drinking beer, reciting Newton Minow's "Great Wasteland" essay. When Jennifer is not around, I unplug the TV and turn it to the wall. Virgil knows the rules, and never asks to have it turned on.

Real life is always more captivating than the artifice of movies and TV. Take my current situation. Just who was Virgil, and why did so many people want him?

Katzenberg/Von Schulte had said the old man was a pedophile and child murderer. Lenora Hart had stated he was a Nazi and killer of Jews (*and* the child murderer). Father Abelard's tale was of a turncoat bank robber who had murdered his pals and disappeared with the money.

I believed none of them. I'd been taken in once by Suzy Anger's lies (Abelard had been right on the money on that point) and wasn't about to fall for any more science fiction until I found out what in the hell was really going on.

But at least I had an answer as to why there were protestors in front of the movie house.

On the screen, I recognized a fat Marlon Brando with cheeks that looked like he'd stuffed toilet paper in them (Not that he really needed to pack something in his face to acquire the look. It seemed to me that the legendary thespian was on his way to becoming a first-class lard-ass). He was mumbling incoherently to a short, Italian-looking gent about "making him an offer he couldn't refuse."

"Bullshit!" hollered somebody in the audience. "You don't make nobody no offer! You take'm for a ride!"

My eyes were drawn to where the voice emanated from. In the movie's flickering light, I saw a man waving a closed fist at the screen. The woman next to him turned and looked furtively behind her, as if she were expecting someone.

Suzy Anger.

Clutching my ersatz dinner, I navigated the aisle and sat at her right. The gesturing man was at her left.

"Popcorn?" I asked, proffering the box of buttered kernels. "Coke?"

"Johnny!" The relief in her voice rang true. "You're okay!" She'd shucked her biker gal garb, and was clothed in a black turtleneck sweater and jeans. Sleek Beatle boots with an obsidian shine. Stunningly Bohemian.

She grabbed my wrist and squeezed. My heart was racing, but I shook her hand off like she had the plague. She gazed at me in surprise, and the hurt in her eyes was real.

The man who had shouted at Brando on the screen leaned over.

"This the guy?" he asked Suzy Anger.

"This is he." (Impeccable pronunciation! She was truly high-class.)

"Johnny," she said. "Meet Angelo 'The Anvil' Boninni."

"The Anvil?" I asked.

He held up a block-like fist. It looked like you could hammer out white-hot horseshoes on its surface.

"The Anvil," he said, grinning.

"You have such nice friends, Suzy," I said.

"I need people like Angelo around me."

"With the circles you run in, I believe it." It was my turn to lean over. "Hey Angelo," I asked. "Do you drive a yellow Dodge Super Bee?"

"You made me, huh?"

"A bright yellow muscle car is not what I'd call the most inconspicuous of vehicles."

"It's stolen. I changed the plates, too. It's all I could come up with in a pinch. Damn thing goes like a bat outta hell, though."

"He work for you?" I asked Suzy Anger.

"He's a friend," she replied. "I asked him to keep an eye on you, to make sure you were safe."

A woman directly behind us tapped me on the shoulder. "Would you please keep it down," she asked. "I can't hear the movie."

The Anvil turned and threw her a cold, murderous stare. She shriveled in her seat.

"Let's get outta here," he said, pointing to the screen, where the little Italian man knelt obsequiously and kissed Brando's hand.

"Ah, crap," said the Anvil disgustedly. "I never kissed nobody's hand. Kissed their ass, maybe. But later, they'd get popped, that's for sure. Who's Brando tryin' to play anyway? The fuckin' Pope? C'mon, let's go."

I followed them into the lobby, where we huddled in a far corner; the cabby, the femme fatale (Abelard's off-handed remark was the perfect description of her) and the ham-handed, block-shouldered hit man. I nibbled popcorn as Angelo Boninni held court.

Complaining about the cliched "Godfather," he was an accumulation of clichés himself. Outfitted in a porkpie hat and sharkskin suit, the Anvil was as out of place in nineteen-seventy-three as a Brylcreemed Sinatra crooning to an audience filled with swooning bobbysoxers. He spoke in a hard-nosed Bronx street patter, gesturing with his hands in the Italian fashion.

"Brando gets a best actor award for hammin' his way through a make-believe role," he said. Most o' the guys in the organization love this movie. I hate it. The real godfathers ain't like that at all. There's them that fetch the cash and them that pockets it. Them that lives and them that dies."

"This is better than the movie," I said to Suzy Anger. "I don't know what's more exciting, your line-up of acquaintances or your tall tales.

"I think it's the tall tales, though," I continued. "Virgil was never any of those things you told me, was he?"

She curled her lower lip and frowned, shaking her head. "No. But I didn't mean to lie to you."

"You said that after the first pack of lies."

"Yes. But it was for a good cause."

"'Them that gets the cash,' you mean?"

The Anvil answered for her. "The money is nothing. It's just a way of keeping score."

"I wasn't talking to you," I said, dismissing him with a flick of my hand. "I want her to answer the question." I pointed an accusatory digit at Suzy.

He took a threatening step toward me. She held him back with the touch of a finger to his barrel chest.

"Down, boy," I said. His hand went to his pocket. Another man with a gun. Well, I wasn't going to scare easy.

I flashed Abelard's twenty-two. "I've got one of those, too."

"Both of you stop it!" she said. "Johnny, you put that gun away. You're drawing attention to us. Angelo, I'm going to tell Johnny exactly what is going on, and why."

I pocketed the pistol and waited silently for her to begin her newest yarn.

"Angelo is an old friend of the family, Johnny," she began. "My father's business partner."

I opened my mouth to interject a question, but she quieted me with a gentle finger on my lips.

"Just listen, please."

The Anvil reached out and grabbed a handful of my popcorn, munching on the kernels as she continued her story.

"My father was very successful at what he did. People feared and respected him. I loved him.

"When I was seven years old, a policeman came to my door and told me--me, mind you--that my father was dead, shot in the head during a bank robbery. He smiled when he told me, the sadistic bastard. I was seven, and my whole world fell apart when he said it, and he got pleasure out of it.

"I didn't know then what my father's business interests were, but after the facts surrounding his death were published in the newspapers, I became a source of ridicule on the playground. Gossip can be vicious, and my mother had to move out of state, taking my brother and me with her. My brother killed himself when he was only nineteen years old. He'd been seeing a psychiatrist for years, and we were told that the circumstances surrounding my father's death were the main contributing factor to his suicidal condition.

"My mother died of a broken heart soon after, and I was left to fend for myself. I was sixteen years old, unloved and unwanted."

The words became difficult for her, and she struggled to maintain her composure.

"I'm telling you all of this not out of self-pity; I abandoned that long ago, but to merely inform you of the seriousness of my quest. It was why I lied to you. I couldn't be sure if you were allied with your roommate, and would be a danger to me. I had to feel you out, to see what you knew. When you bit on the pedophile tale I knew you were clean."

"I passed your litmus test?" I said.

"Yes. I'm sure the priest has told you the details of the circumstances surrounding my father's death. He played along with the lies as long as he saw some value in it for himself. Now that the truth is out, Abelard becomes our most dangerous enemy. That man is no Christian."

A point I could readily agree on.

"Sol Katzenberg?" I asked. "Or Ernst Von Schulte? Which one is it? What about him?"

The Anvil dug another hamhock fist into my popcorn. He ate by popping a single kernel in his mouth at a time. Watching him eat I was reminded of Sampson, the star of the Milwaukee County Zoo; a six hundred pound behemoth of a gorilla who daintily peeled each grape before he ate it, his ferocious face an inscrutable mask as he stared impassively through the curious throngs outside his glass-walled prison.

"Ernst was my first real lover," she said. "He was twenty years older than I, and I was his eager pupil. I
believed in him, trusted him, and told him the story of my father's death and of the missing million dollars.

"Everything between us changed after that. He began to research the newspapers, ask me detailed questions I couldn't possibly answer; trying to discover the whereabouts of the
missing getaway car driver. I left him because of his obsession, but it didn't deter him.

"He became violent, tried to pry the whereabouts of the money from me by slapping me around. That's when I turned to Angelo. My father's best friend."

"I convinced him he shouldn't be doing that." said the hit man with a menacing grin. "Nobody hits my little girl and gets away with it."

Taking the measure of the thuggish Bonnini, I could easily imagine his mano-a-mano session with Von Schulte. Something I was eagerly looking forward to myself. I had to pay the bastard back for drugging me. One of the day's many paybacks I had to deliver.

"Angelo told me that whenever I needed help, to call him. I needed him then, and I need him now," she said.

The Anvil shrugged. "I was in the Milwaukee area on business anyway, so what the hell."

On business. I'd scan the newspapers tomorrow, to see if any bodies were found in the alleyways; if somebody showed up in an emergency room with broken legs, or an unfortunate with cement shoes was fished out of the river.

Suzy Anger continued her tale. "Ernst moved out, but he persisted in his search for the getaway car driver. He was a man possessed."

She paused, biting her lower lip.

"To my amazement he found the driver a few weeks ago, hiding out in your apartment."

I paused for effect. "Lenora Hart?"

She sucked in her breath, gritting her teeth. "That has-been has showed up, has she?"

"She has." I told her Lenora's Nazi tale, and her claim that she was Suzy's 'sister in spirit.'..

"She's no friend of mine. She came out of the woodwork a couple of years ago, and she just invited herself to the party." She bit her lower lip, deep in thought.

"I thought we'd taken care of her, Angelo," she said to the hit man.

"That lady don't scare easy, Suzy," he replied. "Leave her to me. Next time we meet, no more games."

"But she's here now," I said. "And she wants to play."

"I suppose she made a pass at you?" Suzy asked.

Did I detect a hint of jealousy in her voice? "She did, but so did you."

"The difference is that I meant it. Her body's a tool to her, nothing more. That woman would spread her legs for a cheeseburger and fries."

"Forget her for a minute. I have one *big* question," I asked. "How do you know that Virgil didn't spend the money? It's been a long time since this supposed robbery. The money--if it ever existed--could be long gone."

"The money *does* exist, and it's still there; every penny of it."

"But how do you know that?" I shot back. "Did Virgil tell you he still had it?"

"Virgilio," answered the Anvil, swallowing the last of his popcorn. "Virgilio Boninni. My brother, and a traitor. He called me, on and off, over the years. I could never trace the calls, but he told me he never spent the cash. I know Virgilio. He was telling the truth. Every red cent of that million is layin' around somewhere, wherever he hid it."

"Your brother?" I said to the Anvil. "And you side with his enemies?"

Boninni shrugged. "One thing you learn in this business is you stand by your partners or otherwise . . ."

The Anvil never finished the sentence. I heard the "pok!" of a pistol shot as he slumped to the floor, clawing at the red hole in his chest. He raised an arm, extending a finger like Adam to the Creator in Michelangelo's Sistine ceiling.

"Suzy," he moaned as he died. "Get th' hell outta here."

I turned to see Mohammed and Hakeem, standing at the far end of the lobby, pistols capped with silencers pointed in our direction.

The sadistic Hakeem grinned as he leveled his pistol at me. I ducked as the shots whizzed overhead.

Pok! Pok!

I grabbed Suzy Anger's hand and pulled her away from the dead Angelo the Anvil. "Run!" I said, stating the obvious.

The gunmen gave chase, racing toward us across the lobby's frayed Oriental-style carpet. The lone girl behind the counter screamed and flattened herself against the floor as the two passed by, firing as they ran. A stray shot hit the glass display case, scattering a cloud of Goobers and Raisinettes.

We raced through the theater as the Godfather played itself out on the screen, celluloid gunmen shooting down Brando/Vito Corleone in a mob hit; real life gunmen blasting at Suzy Anger and me. Movie patrons, at first confusing the real shots with the on screen gunfire, were unaware as to what was happening; but when the flesh-and-blood shootists were seen popping away, there was a collective scream from the seats. Popcorn boxes flew in the air as customers hit the dirt and we hit the exit doors at the rear of the theater, sprinting down a dark alley to the parking lot and my cab.

We jumped inside as I gunned the engine and raced out of the lot, parking attendant waving at me to stop.

Not now, pal, I thought. Get my license number and call the cops. They'd be a welcome addition.

I blew west down Wisconsin Avenue. Snow was drifting on the streets and sidewalks and traffic was nonexistent. I found the exit for 1-94 and headed south, back toward home. I looked in my rearview. There was no sign of Hakeem and Mohammed in hot pursuit.

"This is it," I told her. "I'm going home, and we're calling the cops."

"Johnny, no!" She grabbed at the wheel and we struggled for it, nearly piling the cab against the on ramp's retaining wall.

"Stop it!" I said, securing control of the wheel.

"You can't go home," she said. "The police will arrest you."

I took my foot off the gas pedal and we coasted onto the highway, merging with sparse traffic.

"Arrest me? Why?"

"Because Ernst Von Schulte's body was discovered in your apartment this afternoon, shot through the heart. The police found a gun next to the body. That gun has your fingerprints on it."

I pulled over to the shoulder. A car whizzed by, the driver angrily honking his horn.

"My prints?" It was like I was plummeting down a bottomless well, looking up toward the light, Suzy Anger hanging over the edge, calling to me.

"*Your* prints, Johnny. Remember a drunk in a tavern a few weeks ago? He tried to sell you a gun?"

It had been at the Kitty Kat Lounge. A scruffy Mexican with a pockmarked face and an addict's pipe cleaner arms was trying to pawn a hot pistol off on me for twenty bucks. He danced that peculiar junkie's hot foot shuffle (the abbreviated shuck-and-jive when they're consumed by the desperate need for a fix), blabbing a mile a minute.

"I told him to butt out."

"But you held the pistol when he tried to force it on you."

I recalled the scene. He'd shoved the gun in my hand.

"It's a good piece, man," he'd said. "Fits your hand, too."

I'd shoved the firearm back. After 'Nam, I never wanted to pull a trigger again. I'd told him so.

"I was set up?"

"That gun was found in your apartment."

"Then all of this has been a set-up?"

"Not all. They were going to try and frighten you into telling them where the money was. That's why they went with the Nazi thing. I want you to know that it wasn't me who tried to rope you with those lies. It was them."

"You went with the Nazi thing."

She lowered her head in shame. "Like I said before, I didn't trust you, either. This has all been the priest's doing."

"Father Abelard?"

"He's a bad man, Johnny."

"You knew him, before today?"

"Yes. His brother was one of my father's best friends. He engineered all of this, Johnny. Starting with the wounding of your roommate. I went along because I had to. He threatened me with the most awful things. I had no choice."

Abelard . . . I began to fantasize about blowing his brains out and leaving his corpse for the hounds to feast on. If he'd been standing in front of me at that very moment, I would have done just that. Then again, I had to think hard on my brief relationship with Suzy Anger. Throughout the course of the day she'd told me a veritable Dagwood Sandwich of tall tales, piled high with truths, half-truths and outright lies, all slathered with slander. The trouble with a woman like Suzy was that I couldn't pick and choose. She was such a damned good liar that I had to swallow the story whole to discern the difference between what was real and what was not real. Was she to be believed about Abelard?

I set the question aside for future debate, deciding instead to take a different tack.

"You mentioned 'wounding' of my roommate," I said. "So Virgil was alive when we found him in the apartment?"

"Yes."

"Who took him?"

"Who knows? Von Shulte. Abelard. They've got him stashed somewhere."

I had a sudden flashback to the scene where Virgil had promised me he was going to pay me back for all my kindness, remembering the second part of our conversation.

"I got the money socked away, Johnny," he'd said. "You just let me know when you want it." Then he'd tossed a furtive sidelong glance, as if giving me a sign as to the location of his buried treasure. I had marked it off as the drunken ravings of an old man, but I now knew the significance of that seemingly casual glance.

The movement with his eyes had been a signal.

I knew where the money was!

Suzy Anger saw the astonished revelation spread across my face.

"What is it, Johnny?" she asked.

"Nothing."

"You know, don't you? Where the money is?"

"No. I'm going home."

"But the police . . ."

"I'll take my chances."

She leaned over and kissed me lightly on the cheek.

I fought my desires and held her at arm's length. "Who killed Von Shulte? Who planted the gun?"

"It was Angelo. You saw me tied to that chair. Angelo found out and went wild. He shot Ernst in his bookstore, and then hauled the body back to your apartment, planted the gun and phoned the police. He thought he'd killed two birds with one stone."

A solitary tear rolled down her cheek. "I didn't know he was going to do it, Johnny. I would never have struck out against you like that."

"What about Angelo? He's stretched out in the theater lobby, died protecting you, and you're showing no remorse."

"Angelo was a big boy. He knew there were inherent dangers involved when I called on him."

I doubted Angelo would have agreed with her. If he could have spoken on his behalf, that is.

"Who shot Virgil?" I asked.

"I don't know. I truly don't." She slid close to me, her breast nuzzled my arm. I felt her nipple grow hard as a button as she rubbed it against me.

She pulled me close and pressed her lips on mine. Her lips parted as her tongue snaked into my mouth. I was in that well again,

falling,

falling,

falling.

She unbuckled my belt and hooked her thumbs into my pants and pulled them down, tugging at them until they lay crumpled around my ankles. Then she did the same with my underwear. She untied her shoes and slid out of her pants and panties.

I eyed the perfect v of her pubic area, like it had been airbrushed by Vargas. She reached between my legs and stroked me.

"Oh, Johnny," she whispered as she flicked her tongue in my ear.

I grabbed her and pulled her on top of me. She opened her legs and moaned as she sat, taking all of me into her. Resting her elbows on my shoulders, she nestled her face in my neck and began riding me slowly.

"Take me, Johnny," she sighed. "Now."

Hi-ho Silver!

I guided her with my hands on her hips as she ground down on me. It didn't take long. A quivering, supercharged sensation snaked down my spine, concentrating its raw power in my testicles. She clamped her teeth onto my neck, drawing blood. I shuddered violently, bared my fangs. She snapped like a whip cord as I came inside her, squeezed the backs of my arms, flexed her neck and cried out in a sing-song ululation--an alien, primeval cadence--as she came with me.

Spent, I watched the snow whip against my windshield, heard the wind alternately sigh and howl as it shook the cab. She snuggled close, pressed her cheek against my chest.

"I can hear your heartbeat," she said.

I cursed silently, pissed off for succumbing so easily. Yet I was supremely satisfied. My body hummed with an electric glow.

"It was fantastic, wasn't it?" she whispered. She pressed her lips against my ear; her breath hot, seductive as she nibbled my lobe.

"Johnny," she said. "I love you."

I dittoed her statement, silently cursing myself for a dumb sonofabitch.

I pulled my pants up and kissed her (slowly, lovingly) a final time before I put the cab into gear, pulled off the shoulder and back onto the highway.

I wasn't falling. I had fallen.

***

The storm was the only bit of good luck I'd had all day.   Pursuit by law enforcement was unlikely, as they had their hands full with fender benders. Which was why we'd also been able to screw full bore on the shoulder of the highway without being nabbed *in flagrante delicto*.

We passed cars that had skidded off the highway and into the ditch, drivers patiently waiting for a tow truck or a state patrol squad.

Prior to our turn-off back to my hometown we spotted a VW bus painted with bright yellow flowers (the once-ubiquitous hippie vehicle of choice now looked tragically dated just a few years after the Summer of Love) stranded in the ditch; engine running, curtains drawn. A few unrepentant hippies, probably blowing dope, waiting for the cops and a tow. A surrealistic anomaly.

I proceeded slowly off the freeway and onto the highway that led back to my factory town home. If the cops did collar me, what was I going to do? Would Suzy Anger back me, tell the truth (If her latest version of events <u>was</u> the truth)?

Max Jacob once asked Picasso why he was so nice with people that didn't really matter and so hard on his friends. Pablo replied, "I don't care about the first group, but since I care very much about my friends, it seems to me I ought to put our friendship to the test every once in a while. Just to make sure it was as strong as it needed to be."

Suzy Anger certainly wasn't my friend, but she professed love and if the law did indeed grab me I would put her to Picasso's test.

I prayed she'd pass it.

Yes, dammit, I'd been a fool. But *something* in her awakened *something* in me. Maybe it was her recognition of "Les Demoiselles d'Avignon" in my cab those many long hours ago. Her look of utter helplessness when I spotted her tied to that chair in Katzenberg's book shop.

Or her sculptured emerald eyes. The flush in her cheek like softly dappled strokes from Renoir's brush. The Renaissance sensuality of her full lips.

The silky elegance of her pubic hair. The cloying quality of her sex as she wrapped her legs around me and slowly sucked me in.

She was an electric presence; a magnet that drew me inexorably to her. I no more wanted to resist her than resist my need to paint.

***

I drove past sagging century-old factories, many of them working full swing. Tricky Dick Nixon may have been evil incarnate as the McGovernites had insisted, but times were good and the money was flowing.

Hell, we were still dropping tons of bombs in 'Nam. Everyone knows that pockets jingle in wartime.

Except when you're on the losing side and although it looked like we were going to take the fall in this fight, America was too goddamned huge, too powerful, to suffer any economic consequences of getting our asses kicked by a nation the size of New England and with a Nineteenth Century economy.

Suffer anywhere but in our collective soul, and you could see evidence of that everywhere. There was a mean-spirited dispiritedness to America these days; a "hooray for me and the hell with everybody" war cry that I wanted no part of. The sweet milk of the American dream had gone sour in the bottle.

I steered the cab into the alley behind my apartment, parking it.

"Wait here," I told her.

"The police . . ." she said, clutching my arm.

"I'll take my chances." I took her hand off my bicep, leaned over and kissed her. I stepped outside. The wind nearly knocked me over, icy snow peppering my face as I made my way to the steps.

If the cops were truly going to bust me, they could do it here and now. If not, I was going to play this drama out to the end.

Clutching the hand rail and fighting the powerful wind, I slowly climbed the steps to my door.

If Suzy Anger's tale of murder and set-up were true, there probably would have been one of two things greeting me: a cop posted to prevent entry to the crime scene, or a padlock on my door in place of the cop.

There was neither. I opened the door and stepped inside.

It was exactly as I had left it less than twenty-four hours earlier. Neat and sparsely furnished, the TV stood facing the corner like the dunce that it was, the Starr's Jewelers clock hummed on the wall. No marks of police investigation (dusting for prints, collection of evidence samples), which is what I would have expected to find if Von Schulte's body had in fact been dumped on my floor and later discovered. This, combined with the lack of a cop as a sentinel or padlock on my door, was irrefutable evidence that I had been handed another (and I vowed my last) lie from Suzy Anger.

I cursed myself (again!) for a fool as I stood in the open doorway.

I paused, surveying my apartment with a critical eye.

Something *was* awry. Maybe it was the cushions on the sofa, which seemed just a hair out of place; or the clock, which hung a bit off kilter.

The apartment had been tossed, and by experts. They had been searching for what I was sure I was going to find in a few minutes: the key to the whereabouts of Virgil's fabled million dollars.

I jumped nervously as my refrigerator kicked in, clanking, and then sighing like a tired old engine.

I walked across the room to the kitchen, where I had sat at the table with Virgil and he had motioned with his eyes.

I thought back again to that moment. I was positive he'd been signaling me. I just wasn't sure of where or what he had been pointing to.

A quick look was all it would take. If I was correct in my assumption, I would have solved the puzzle.

But then what? I would still have murderers and thieves to contend with, and once they knew that I knew where the money was, all bets would be off and Johnny Jump would have a half-life of about three minutes.

I opened the kitchen door and went straight to what I thought was Virgil's hiding place. The life-sized portrait of the old man that I had been working on sat on my oversized easel, and the room smelled of linseed oil, paint and turp. I stared into the bright painted eyes, questioning them, wondering if my hunch was correct.

I looked. It was.

I felt my heart thumping in my chest as I realized that there was a germ of truth in all of the tall tales I'd been told in the past few hours and that my hunch had been on the money. The million dollars, at least, was real.

And I alone had the clue to its hiding place.

The clanking began again, and after a long three seconds I realized it wasn't the refrigerator. I held my breath and strained to hear who or what it was.

Someone else was in the apartment.

My kitchen window looked out over the alley. I parted the curtains and looked down. Through the driving snow I studied Suzy Anger's silhouette in the cab. Steam created by her body heat fogged the windows. Gray smog puffed from the tailpipe. The wipers slapped back and forth with the monotony of a metronome.

I pulled back from the window, jerked my head around.

I had heard another small sound; somebody whispering a nearly inaudible curse.

It didn't take a rocket scientist to realize that whoever it was in the apartment was not a benign presence.

I drew the twenty-two, my finger tight on the trigger. This time it was for real. I was going to use the gun on whomever it was who had violated my home.

I snapped off the light switch in the kitchen and reached around the wall and found the switch controlling the overhead lights in the living room and turned that off, too.

My friend and I were now in total darkness, but I had the advantage. I knew the layout of the turf.

I squatted down with my back against the wall, revolver in hand, and waited.

It didn't take long. There was a muffled thump, and then an angry curse as my uninvited guest barked his shins against my sofa. I stood and pointed the pistol where I had heard the sound.

"Stay where you are!" I commanded.

Blam! came the response as the intruder opened up with a heavy automatic, punching a hole in the wall six inches from my ear. I dropped and rolled, firing in the direction of the gun's report.

Tak! Tak!

The twenty-two sounded like a large rubber band being snapped.

Blam!

Tak!

I heard a grunt and a thud as my assailant fell to the floor, followed by labored breathing. I waited a full minute before sliding up the wall and flicking the light switch.

A man lay on the floor on the other end of my living room, his chest heaving. I crept up to him, twenty-two pointed at his head, to see who it was I had hit.

Ernst Von Schulte.

The same hombre Suzy Anger said had been found dead in my apartment earlier in the day.

Not so deceased, however, that he couldn't squeeze two shots off at me.

I had hit him with all three rounds. One had creased his left eye, a second pierced his cheek. I saw a tiny hole dripping blood in his chest where I'd banged him with the third round.

He was dying and he knew it.

"Nice shooting," he wheezed. "I didn't think you had it in you."

"I can handle a gun as well as the next guy."

Wincing in pain, he said, "I could've shot you as you came through the door."

"Why didn't you?"

"I wanted to see if you knew where the money was."

His good eye questioned mine.

"You know, don't you?" he said.

"Yes. Just now."

He smiled. "Ah. Good. You keep it for yourself. Too many people have died for it. You show your hand, and you'll die, too."

He began to pant, like a long distance runner at the end of a race.

"You keep your eye out for Suzy, you hear?" he said.

I knelt at his side and took his hand in mine, priest to confessor. "I will."

"And you watch your own behind, too. Don't trust her too much. Look what happened to me."

His eyes began to film over with a glassy sheen.

"But it was sweet while it lasted. Ask me if it was worth it."

I humored the dying man. "Was it?"

He flashed a grin that spread across his face. "Fuckin' A."

He reached up with his free hand and grabbed at the air, pulling down whatever illusory object he had snatched, clutching it to his chest.

"Keep your pecker up, Johnny Jump," he said. He squeezed my hand. His head lolled to one side, his good eye rolled in its socket and he yawned as he exhaled his last breath.

I felt his neck for a pulse. He was dead, and I had killed him. All those rounds I'd fired in 'Nam, and most of the time I never knew what or who I'd hit. Now, as a civilian, I'd scored my first certifiable body count.

"Sorry, pardner," I said as I pocketed my twenty-two and Von Schulte's forty-five.

Since this crazy day began I had been in two firefights, a high-speed highway shoot-out, screwed in full view on the freeway, hijacked my employer's automobile and had never even *seen* one cop.

By rights, I should have been in jail, sans shoelaces and belt, awaiting trial on a variety of felony charges. The fact that I wasn't could have been a subject for Dali's surrealistic brush.

It had been a remarkable turn of luck (good or bad, I really couldn't say) but I wasn't about to try and change it by leaving Von Schulte sprawled on my apartment floor.

I rolled his body up in my faux oriental rug, hoisted it over my shoulder and hauled it out of the apartment down the steps, where I tossed it into the cab's trunk.

Suzy Anger eyed me in the rearview mirror. If she knew what I had in the rug, or what I was doing, she betrayed no emotion.

"What was that you put in the trunk?" she asked as I slid behind the wheel.

"Just taking out the garbage," I said as I pulled out of the alley.

I remembered Von Shulte's dying words. He had warned me not to trust her too much.

As if I needed the advice. She'd burned me once too often in the course of this day. But I wanted answers; from her and the other players in this sick little drama. Therefore, I'd play her game just a while longer.

Plus, I now had *two* pistols snuggled in my pockets.

I knew that before this night was over, there'd be more bodies littering the landscape.

I just hoped one of them wouldn't be mine.

PART SIX:
8:01 P.M. – Midnight

Think of it as a Punch and Judy show. Or an aberrant *Commedia del Arte.*

We were all of us puppets; me, Von Schulte, Virgil, the Nazi bikers, Lenora Hart, Abelard and his Black Panther hit men, Angelo "the Anvil" Boninni.

And there was no doubt as to who was pulling the strings.

That Suzy Anger was a world-class liar also wasn't in dispute. She'd taken me in (and everyone else, it seems) in major league style.

That she was seductive and extremely dangerous was also a given. I felt like a male black widow spider as I sat next to her in the cab. Inexorably drawn to that which I knew would mate with me, then calmly sink her poisonous fangs into me and devour my shriveled remains.

We sat in the alleyway, the cab's heater hissing, wipers smudging the snow on my windshield.

"Where to now?" I asked.

She stared straight ahead, face impassive as if it had been chiseled from granite.

"What did you put in the trunk?" she asked again.

The howling wind and laboring of the cab's engine had muffled the sounds of the firefight that had taken place in my apartment just a few moments before. If she knew Von Schulte was waiting in ambush for me, she certainly hid it well.

"Your friend Von Schulte."

"He's dead?"

"He didn't climb inside by himself."

"You really killed him? Why?"

"Why don't you tell me? It was you who had him wait in ambush for me, wasn't it?"

She shrugged her shoulders in resignation. Then suddenly, the truth was revealed.

"Ernst had become a liability," she said.

"So you coerced him into murdering me?"

"Oh, Johnny! I knew he couldn't take you. You're one of the most resourceful men I've ever met."

"Uh huh. I imagine you used that same line on Von Schulte. Pit two of your lovers against each other. Like betting on every horse in the race. Whichever one crosses the finish line, you're in the money."

"No, Johnny!"

"Please don't continue to insult my intelligence, Suzy. Just point me in the right direction."

"There's a house on the lake," she said, gesturing south. "Near the Illinois line. Your friend Virgil is there. Alive."

Virgil, she said. Alive.

"Who else?" I asked.

"Nobody, maybe. Everybody."

"Is this it, Suzy? The final act?"

"Yes."

The night had grown black, like a cancer. The swirling snow was blinding as I maneuvered out of downtown and onto Sheridan Road, heading south. And who did I see for the first time, now that I didn't need or want them? The cops!

A police prowl car crawling in the opposite direction shined its spotlight on my cab and stopped me. I rolled down the window as we sat side by side, the cop car facing north, my cab south. Had Sparky phoned me in as gone missing with his cab? I'd find out in a second or two.

I knew the cop in the passenger seat. Gary Stahl. A good guy most of the time, he'd let most minor infractions slide.

He rolled his window down. "Johnny Jump," he said. "You working tonight?"

"Got called in, Gary," I said. "Johnny Torelli's wife is having a baby."

"No kiddin'? That's great. Tough luck for you, though." He shined the spotlight past me, onto Suzy Anger's face.

"Fare?" he asked.

"Yeah. On our way to Illinois." And I shot it out with somebody a few minutes ago and I've got his body stuffed in the trunk and I'm packing two pistols, both of which could probably be tied to a half-dozen homicides each.

"Well, be careful. There's been a couple of good accidents tonight already."

He motioned to his partner, a flush-faced kid in an oversized cop hat.

"Talk about tough luck," he said. "This is Phil's first night on the job."

I leaned over the wheel. "Good luck, Phil," I said to the rookie.

"Yeah," said the kid, never looking at me. He had a pimply complexion, and his uniform collar loosely circled his scrawny neck.

"See ya," said Gary Stahl, rolling up his window as the squad pulled away.

"See ya, Gary," I said.

I put the cab in gear and proceeded slowly down the center of Sheridan Road.

"That was close," said Suzy Anger, breathing a sigh of relief.

"Not really. Most of the cops in this town know me, and they know I bend the law a little every once in a while, but I never break it. Not until today, that is."

"When this is all over and we have the money, you and I can go away to somewhere. You can paint all you want, and never worry about having to make a living."

She didn't have a clue. Making a living was what it was all about. Whether as a plumber, electrician, bank teller, cop, cab driver or portrait painter.

"I couldn't live like that, Suzy. For me, painting *is* living. It's life itself."

"I didn't mean it that way," she said, but her words rang hollow.

She now knew that I knew she was a cheat and a liar, and responsible for the deaths of at least two men and God knows how many more.

At least I had the heavy comfort of Von Schulte's forty-five and Abelard's twenty-two buried in my coat pockets.

I had killed Von Schulte, and I would kill again if I was threatened.

I was sure I would be.

***

The southeast end of town transmogrified from concrete and blacktop into stretches of native prairie criss-crossed with lonely dirt roads used by Chicago hit men to dump their handiwork, young lovers to consummate unbridled passion and gonzo dope heads looking to score a buzz.

At Suzy's direction I drove along First Avenue, which hugged the lake. There was a series of homes built between the road and the lake (which was roaring in all its fury, towering gray waves crashing against the shoreline).

The homes were grouped in blocks of threes, constructed where there was enough space between the road and the lake to accommodate a lot and tiny yard. We passed by a half dozen of these blocks as the lake tossed curtains of icy spray over the houses and onto the road. My headlights illuminated stark branches of trees glazed with ice that shined like sugar candy. I pushed the cab at a snail's pace, wipers on high, headlights on low beam, peering through the snow and spray and hoping another car wouldn't be headed towards us, as blind as we were.

The angry wind bent willow, pine and cottonwood trees at crazy angles. The storm was becoming so violent that I began to think about turning back, away from the lake and approaching our destination from a different angle.

"There," said Suzy, pointing to a ranch-style pink frame home that appeared out of the storm. "That's it."

I parked next to the home. The Super Bee sat alone in the driveway. We'd have company, and I was positive I could guess who some, if not all, of them would be.

The house sat perched on a tiny peninsula, assaulted by the lake from east, south and north. There was less than twenty-five feet of land between the lake and the home in all directions. Huge waves crashed with ominous force against the shore as the hard, cold wind bore down on us from the north.

Clutching collars to our throats, we raced to the front door. Suzy rang the bell. A light appeared in the front window behind drawn shades.

Father Abelard opened the door. He looked at me in mild surprise.

"Johnny Jump," he said, sounding as if he were impressed by my presence.

"Thought I'd be dead, didn't you, Father?" I said as I followed Suzy Anger inside.

"That possibility had occurred to me," he said as he closed the door behind us. "I must admit, you've been quite a surprise to all of us. Sort of like the fabled cat with nine lives."

"Who is 'us?'" I asked.

"You haven't figured that out yet?"

"No, but I think I'm getting close to the truth."

"I would have expected nothing less from you, Johnny Jump."

"Enough," said Suzy with amazing authority, shaking snow off her coat. "Are they all here?"

"They are," said the father. "I daresay that Mr. Jump's appearance is going to be quite a shock to them, though."

"Why?" I interjected. "Was I supposed to be bumped off in my apartment? After Von Schulte pried whatever information I had out of me?"

"That was, I think, the plan," said Abelard. "Where is Ernst, by the way?"

"Dead. In the trunk of my cab. I punched three holes in him with your twenty-two."

A grudging admiration lit the priest's eyes, but not one whit of Christian sorrow for the loss of an unrepentant soul.

"So, Suzy," he said, turning his attention to her. "How are you going to handle this sudden change in agenda?"

She tossed her coat on the threadbare living room sofa. "There's no change. We'll just have to cut Johnny in, that's all. Did you wipe the Dodge of prints?"

"The car's clean." Abelard pursed his lips and shook his head slowly. "You're going to be very unpopular, Suzy, by cutting Johnny in. He's a late comer. Someone with no personal involvement."

"We have no choice," she said. "He knows where the money is, and we don't. Unless you shook it out of the old man."

"Not hardly. He's a tough old bird. Hakeem and Mohammed used a little 'creative interrogation' with lit cigarettes on Methuselah's feet. He didn't spill a thing."

Suzy Anger turned to me. Her eyes were cold and uncompromising.

"Okay, Johnny," she said. "You know most everything. It's not a pleasant story, but you're a big boy and I doubt you're surprised."

"I know nothing," I replied. "But I want to know *why* did people have to die?"

"Why? For the money, that's why," offered Abelard.

"No!" she shot back. "Not for the money. Nothing was for the money."

"I doubt you could convince our compatriots of that," said the priest.

I looked around the empty room. "Who else is here?"

"Some old acquaintances, some new," said Abelard.

"Follow me," said Suzy, ushering me into a large kitchen; so large, in fact, it seemed to occupy nearly half the house.

All sat at a family-size nineteen-fifties style pink Formica and chrome kitchen table. The good Father took a chair next to Black Panthers Hakeem and Mohammed, in full Panther regalia of tams, shades and short puffy 'fros. A woman with a hatchet face peppered with acne scars sat at Abelard's left. Next to her sat Lenora Hart, absently puffing on a Virginia Slims, and at her immediate left was a doe-eyed man with a pale pear-shaped face and a cochineal explosion of hair that erupted from his temples like Bozo the Clown.

Each nursed a bottle of Falstaff beer, and each (including the priest) had a revolver on the table, like they were at a poker game in an old Wild West movie. The black hats waiting to shoot it out with the alabaster chapeaued sheriff.

I had the gut-wrenching feeling that the sheriff was going to be played by me.

"Sit," commanded Suzy. I obeyed her. She took the seat at the head of the table, her pistol-packing disciples ringing her like a perverse interpretation of Leonardo's "Last Supper."

"I see you managed to worm your way here, Lenora," said Suzy. "How did you get Ernst to sneak you back into our little group, as if I didn't know?"

"Ernst said sleeping with you was like sleeping with a snake, darling," replied Lenora. "He was afraid you'd have him killed someday. He also said you were a lousy lay." She made a big show of looking around the room, as if Von Schulte would pop out of the cupboards, or suddenly poke his head around a door jamb, to verify her story..

"And I see he's not here," she added. "So I guess his worst fears were realized."

The insults rolled off Suzy's back. "Be careful, Lenora," she said. "There's no love lost between you and anyone here. You don't belong, dear. You're not one of us."

"Thank God for *that*," said Lenora.

I made a show of setting the twenty-two on the table, leaving Von Schulte's forty-five tucked in my pocket. Better to keep my ace in the hole buried with this murderer's row.

The clown laughed, snorting obscenely through his nose. He busied himself rolling a joint from a lid of grass next to his pistol.

He eyed my tiny pistol. "Got a real *player* here, huh Suzy?" His pearl-handled long-barreled thirty-eight looked obscenely huge compared to my pathetic little twenty-two.

"He killed Von Schulte," said Abelard. "With that gun."

"Really?" said the redhead, staring at me with a combination of curiosity and contempt. "This fuckin' hippie took out Ernst?"

Hippie?, I thought. Fuck him. I told him so. "Fuck you, asshole," I said. Not exactly a quote from the pages of *belles-lettres*, but in this case and with an obvious pea-brain like him I figured I had made my point.

His fingers snaked towards his gun. Abelard clamped a hand on his wrist.

"Stop it, Jack," said the priest.

"I'll take care of this narcoleptic assassin for the establishment later," said Jack, spouting the incomprehensible megalomania of the degenerated 'revolution.'

Suzy sighed impatiently. "Let's get this over with."

"Too much Marxist rhetoric and LSD," Abelard whispered to me, nodding at Jack, who eyed me with a glare that said 'we'll finish this later, bub.'

"Get this over is right," said the hatchet-faced woman. "Sexist pigs."

"Shut the fuck up Elaine, you bitch," retorted Hakeem. "Or this 'sexist pig' is gonna waste your bulldyke ass."

Lenora Hart threw her head back and laughed. "Lordy, lordy," she chuckled, clapping her hands. "What a divine comedy!"

Suzy Anger leveled a cold stare at her. If looks could kill, I thought.

"All of you shut up," chided Suzy Anger. "We have a situation here that has to be resolved."

All went silent and looked to Suzy, who sat like chairman of the board of this group of misfits.

"Johnny will have to be cut in on the deal," she said.

"Fuck you!" said Hakeem, leaping to his feet.

"I'm afraid my brother takes exception to cutting in our half black-ass friend here," said Mohammed. "I concur with his assessment."

I pulled my gun closer. This wasn't going to be a droll Dorothy Parker/H. L. Mencken/Algonquin dinner table conversation of parrying wits.

The slings and arrows tossed here were going to be real, fired from the various artillery displayed on the table top.

"He knows where the money is, and we don't" said Suzy. "You have any better suggestions?"

Hakeem raised a hand and popped open a wicked-looking stiletto. He slowly removed his sunglasses and leveled deadly brown-button eyes at me.

"Yeah, *I* got a better suggestion," he said. "I carve a piece outta his one-quarter-black-ass. He'll tell us what we want to know."

"You couldn't force it out of the old man," she said. "What makes you think you can do any better with him?"

"He's a sissy," said Hakeem. "I can see it in his eyes."

I'd had enough. "Look, asshole," I said. "I didn't spend a year in-country in 'Nam, dodging AK47 rounds, mortar barrages, land mines and pungi sticks just to get wasted by a sicko like you. Anytime you want to try me, I'm right here."

"Macho bullshit," said Elaine.

"I think Hakeem and Mohammed would appreciate it if you knocked off the feminist litanies, Elaine," said the priest.

""Me, too. I've had my fill of that bilge," said Lenora Hart.

"Johnny gets a cut. That's the way it is. End of discussion," said Suzy Anger. "Anybody who wants to dispute that can leave this room right now and walk out that front door. Or fuck with me later."

There was a thick, menacing tension in the room. Hakeem placed the knife on the table, sat and slipped his shades back on as Father Abelard fired up a cigarette.

"Someone explain to me what's going on," I said, breaking the ominous silence. "And where is Virgil?"

Suzy Anger motioned to Abelard with a flick of her head.

"You tell him," she said.

"It's a long story," said Abelard, addressing me. "You've heard it before, an abbreviated version."

"I've got a lot of time on my hands, father," I replied, speaking to the priest but keeping a wary eye on the switchblade-wielding Hakeem.

Abelard sucked on his cigarette and released the smoke slowly. He sipped at his beer, tearing contemplatively at the corner of the bottle's label.

"It's a story of four friends," he began slowly. "Tough kids who grew up in Chicago in the shadow of Comiskey Park. Kids who had to punch their way to adulthood, played fast and loose with the law. But friends always. Until one betrayed the others.

"The four friends had made a pact. 'All for one and one for all,' borrowing from *The Three Musketeers*. They were street kids, like I said. They began their careers in crime in the late nineteen-thirties. Petty theft, mostly. But as they grew they graduated to stick-ups, burglary and some extortion.

"They were very successful at what they did, and eluded capture; or even detection for that matter. They were all family men, good providers and good fathers. Well-respected. Their families knew nothing of their criminal enterprises."

"But one of them turned traitor," interjected Suzy Anger.

"Your roommate, Virgil," said the priest. "The friends had planned a brilliant daylight bank robbery. It was going to be the biggest hit they had made to date. Over one hundred thousand dollars. Or so they thought."

"The bank was a drop-off point for Chicago mob money," said Suzy. "They would launder it through legitimate accounts for a slight percentage, returning clean money to mob-fronted businesses."

"There was over a million dollars in untraceable cash the day the friends hit that bank," continued Abelard. "None of the friends knew the bank was mob-affiliated. None except one, that is . . ."

"Virgil," I said, finishing the sentence.

"He knew about the bank's mob connections through his brother, Angelo," said Abelard.

"And you two killed Angelo," said Suzy Anger, glaring at Hakeem and Mohammed. "That was not supposed to be part of the plan."

"Tough titty," retorted Mohammed, lapsing from his impeccable King's English into faux ghetto patter.

"He was in the wrong place at the wrong time," said Hakeem.

Jack fired up his joint and sucked a short hit, holding the smoke deep in his lungs.

"The seeds of a heartless bureaucracy," he spouted as he exhaled, coughing up sweet smoke. "Anybody want a hit?"

No one accepted his offer. "I'll Bogart it, then." He shrugged his shoulders and took another glassy-eyed toke, content in his Maoist dream world.

Abelard continued his story. "Virgil was the getaway driver. The other three, the pistoleros; they hit the bank, stuffed the cash in two duffel bags and hopped in the getaway car."

"Where they were shot by their friend, who took the cash and disappeared," said Suzy Anger.

"End of story?" I asked.

"No," said Abelard. "The mob figured all the friends had collectively planned to rip them off. They retaliated by going after the friends' families."

"Everyone in this room was affected," said Suzy Anger.

"They might as well have killed our mother and little brother," said Elaine, nodding to Jack.

"*My* mother," retorted Jack, jerking a thumb at his sister. "I disinherited that bitch years ago."

"We'll settle that score someday," said Elaine.

"Soon," deadpanned Jack. The two stared at each other in icy hatred.

"Virgil shot my father," said Suzy Anger.

"And my big brother," said Abelard. "I worshipped him, and he shot him down like a dog. Elaine and Jack lost their father in that getaway car, too." He motioned to the siblings. "We're all children of that tragedy."

"So that's what this is all about?" I said. "Revenge?"

"Precisely," answered Abelard.

Lenora Hart held a hand in the air, like a kid in a classroom. "With the exception of me," she said. "I have no axe to grind. I am here strictly for the cash."

"We'll discuss *that* later on," Suzy shot back.

I gestured to the Panthers. "What about them?" I asked the priest.

"A bank guard was killed during the holdup. Not by the murdered friends, but by Virgil as he made his escape."

"Our father," said Mohammed bitterly. "An honest, decent man. Shot dead by a honky motherfucker."

I thought of the gentle old man who had bunked with me for the past two years, and of the lives he had destroyed. He had been two men: one a cold-blooded killer, the other a harmless old drunk. I couldn't reconcile the two.

"We made a pact shortly after our fathers, mothers and siblings were killed," said Suzy Anger. "We've been searching for Virgil for twenty years. Now we've found him."

"And you can exact your revenge," I said. "There was no need to try and con me with those phony Nazi and pedophile stories to discover if I knew where the money was if all you wanted was a payback for your families' misfortunes. In fact, you had Virgil already. There was no need to involve me in anything, was there?"

"The elaborate ruses were all her idea," said the priest, pointing to Suzy Anger. "Cornball melodrama. She thought she could finesse the situation. She researched your background, created the scenarios and we played them out in hopes you would turn on your friend and tell us where the money was. She wanted no blood to be shed. Ha!"

"Only everything went wrong," countered Suzy. She aimed an accusatory finger at Lenora Hart. "This bitch hustled her way into the action, dropped *my* Nazi story on Johnny, and then got in a shooting match with the bikers."

"The Nazi story was part of the plan, wasn't it?" countered Lenora. "And as for the bikers, you could have called off your dogs anytime you wanted to. They fucked with me, they died" She paused, then added icily, "*Anybody* who fucks with me, dies."

Another point I could readily agree on.

As the accusations flew, I felt the house trembling like it had gone weak in the knees. The storm was battering the earth bermed beneath the flimsy structure, and I heard what I thought was the sound of nails separating from studs. The house was in a battle with the elements, and it seemed to me that Ma Nature was winning. No one else, however, seemed to notice.

Ignoring Lenora Hart's thinly-veiled threat, Suzy confronted the priest. "Then your goons decided to shoot down Angelo," she said, glaring at the Panthers. "They'll pay for that later."

"And your man Von Schulte blew that goofy kidnap gambit with that melodramatic girl-tied-to-a-chair scheme," shot back Abelard. "Screwed up that phony robbery at George Webb's. *And* fouled up the ambush at Johnny's apartment."

"Hey man," said Jack, contemplating the smoldering joint he pinched between finger and thumb. "I scored the base of operations in the deserted area, like you asked. Looks like I'm the only one who hasn't fucked up."

"Some house." Elaine winced as a wave smashed against the aluminum siding. "What the hell is happening?"

"Be cool, Sis," said Jack contemptuously. "Everything's copacetic."

"You should never have let that idiot rent this house," I said to Suzy. "All the locals know how unstable this shoreline is. The lake can kick up a major tantrum in a matter of minutes, like what's happening right now. We could be sitting ass-deep in water very shortly, if we don't get the hell out of here."

"You mean the whole *house* could sink in the lake?" asked Elaine, now visibly concerned.

"That's what I said."

"Bull," countered her brother. "I scouted this crib. It's stable. Nothing will happen."

"Says you," I replied. "It's only you Illinois folks who pay top dollar for vanishing shoreline. A fine lot of thieves you are. Ha!"

Suzy Anger fumed, staring at me in mute reply. It was time for me to try and take control of the situation.

"Why didn't you believe me?" I asked her. "I told you I didn't know anything about any money. I told you the truth."

"Because a liar believes everyone else is a liar," interjected the priest. "She has to, to maintain any shred of dignity, or she realizes what a piece of trash she really is."

"The same with a thief," she shot back. "You robbed me of my childhood. Mr. Man of God."

"Sins of the flesh," giggled Jack. "Violating little girls. Say three Our Fathers and three Hail Marys, Abelard. Penance, baby."

"Shut up, you idiot," countered the priest. "Nobody believes those psychotic accusations."

"Not like you, Jack, right?" said Elaine to her brother. "Sneaking in on little sister when everyone was asleep. Night after night for years?" She looked at me, face screwed in intense hatred. "All men are bastards," she hissed.

Lenora Hart giggled. "The family that lays together, stays together." I couldn't believe what I was hearing.

The priest turned his attention to Suzy. "And you," he said. "How many perished, believing they were defending you?"

"Stop it!" I shouted. The room went silent. "I've been sitting here, listening to all of you bandy about accusations and counter-accusations like a pack of fools. You make me want to vomit."

"How about we make you want to *die*?" said Hakeem.

"Always the tough guy, huh?" I said.

"Lighten up, man," said Jack to me. "We're talking about one million dollars here."

"One million dollars can be a great equalizer," said Abelard, tapping down a cigarette on his wrist before lighting it.

"You people killed for *money*?" I said. "Money that wasn't even yours?"

"That money *is* ours, man," said Jack. "We earned it."

"So it *is* the money," I said.

"No argument from me on that point," said Lenora Hart.

"And you," I said to her. "What happened to that principled lady who defended her sisters in court? Fought for the cause?"

"What happened?" she shot back. "I won a few big cases, and got paid diddly for them. Got my face on the cover of TIME, but no law firm wanted to touch me. I was a controversial commodity, too hot to handle. I'm sick and tired of being principled and broke, sitting in a third-floor walk-up office, waiting for the phone to ring. I want my cut of the million. That's all that matters to me now."

"Poor baby," Suzy Anger clucked, but there was no pity in her voice.

"It isn't only the money. It's for justice, too," said Mohammed. "For an innocent black man. For all black people everywhere."

"Fuck that noise," hissed Hakeem. "It's the fuckin' *money*. Where is it?"

"First give me Virgil," I said. "Then we'll talk about the money."

"Uh, uh. He owes us, baby," said Jack.

"You're in no position to make any demands, Johnny," said Suzy Anger. "We want Virgil *and* the money. No deals."

"Then no cash," I replied. Seven pairs of murderous eyes were trained on me. I had made my decision, and it was cast in stone. I wasn't leaving without Virgil. One thing I've learned in life is that you stand by your friends, no matter what transgressions they may have committed. And it was *Virgil* who was my friend, not these sociopathic assholes.

Besides, all I had was the collective word of the murderer's row at the kitchen table that Virgil was indeed a killer. Not exactly what you could take to the bank.

"So," I said after what seemed to be an interminable silence. "What's it going to be?"

As if in answer to my question, a low moan emanated from somewhere in the home. The guttural howl of an animal in great pain. It sent a shiver up my spine.

"Who was that?" I asked. "*What* was that?"

A giant of a man crammed himself into the kitchen. He had to duck to prevent from striking his lion-like head on the lintel and turn sideways to fit his bulk through the doorway. He wore a blue jean jacket with a gaudy Stars and Bars Confederate flag stitched across the back. His barrel-like belly hung over his belt, and thick black hairs carpeted the backs of his hands. Looking over the seven of us sitting at the table, he shook his head in disgust.

"Damn!" he said. "But that old bastard's tough!" He displayed a pair of pliers for all to see. Wedged in its jaws was a yellowed molar, bleeding from its long roots.

I now knew my roommate was somewhere in the house. He was alive, but probably not for much longer. How in the hell would I get us out of here?

The giant smiled broadly, flashing a picket fence grin of piano key teeth. "Couldn't get a word out of'm."

"Meet 'Fat,' Johnny," said Father Abelard. "I believe you were introduced to his brother, Axel, earlier this afternoon."

The resemblance was remarkable. Fat and Axel had obviously been birthed in the identical primordial ooze.

"The late, great Axel, you mean?" I answered.

Fat tossed the pliers. The tooth hit the linoleum and bounced twice, settling in a corner. He pointed at me. "This the nigger sumbitch killed my brother?"

A series of waves slammed into the house in quick succession, and I felt the room pitch slightly. Armageddon, I felt, was close at hand; either with the tempest outside, or with the Neanderthal slime in front of me.

"The 'nigger sumbitch' who killed your brother was one of his biker brothers," I replied angrily. I looked at the Panthers. They sat impassively, impervious to Fat's racist ratings. Nazi bikers were obviously okay to them, but not "mongrels" like me.

There was a sickening crunch of something solid and massive hitting the house, and I felt the floor shift under my feet. The beer bottles tipped and sloshed their contents across the table top. Jack cursed as he slapped at the beer that had splashed across his lap.

Suzy Anger ran to the window. "Jesus!" she shouted. "The shoreline's gone!"

Elaine stood, stabbing her pistol at her brother. "I knew it, you stupid sonofabitch!" she shouted. "You'd fuck up a wet dream!"

"Put the gun down, sis," said Jack, suddenly very cool. "Shooting me isn't going to change anything."

"Shoot him," said Hakeem. "One less to split the cash with."

She lowered the gun slowly. "Not now," she said. "Not here. Plenty of time for that later."

"Plenty," echoed Jack.

I joined Suzy at the window. As I had predicted might happen, the lake had torn away the twenty-five feet of fragile shoreline and the house now sat totally exposed on its east end to the fury of the crashing waves. A huge breaker roared down on us out of the swirling snow and smashed against the home. The structure shifted, tilting to port like a ship without power. It shuddered as a series of smaller waves butted against it.

The house teetered on the dirt and sand precipice. One more big wave and we would be swept into the lake.

"We're going in!" I warned. I moved toward the living room door and to the bedroom beyond where I was sure I would find my friend.

Fat stepped between the doorway and me, blocking my exit with his bulk.

"Where the hell you think you're going?" he asked.

I pulled Von Schulte's forty-five, stepping back out of the range of his massive paws.

"Move it," I said. "Or lose it." (I get so goddamned poetic in perilous situations!)

An electric jolt erupted in the back of my leg. I whirled and saw Hakeem standing at the table, his arm outstretched, index finger pointing in my direction. I looked to where he was pointing, and saw his stiletto quivering in the belly of my thigh. I yanked it out and tossed the blade on the floor.

I felt no pain, only anger and determination; the adrenalin rush of desperation in war. For all their tough-guy rhetoric and posturing, it was the one thing I had over everyone in the room. I had seen combat in all its heinous fury, and I was sure they hadn't.

It was like I had been transported back to 'Nam, surrounded by the enemy, forced to shoot my way out.

I wiped the grin off Hakeem's face with the first shot from my pistol then turned to meet Fat, who roared in outrage and rushed me, arms outstretched like a great grizzly bear.

I pumped two shots into his chest from less than ten feet. He went down face first, crashing like a redwood onto the linoleum.

A second big wave hit the house, and I heard the groan of nails being pulled from studs as we slid closer to the precipice.

The lights flickered, but stayed on.

Jack grabbed for his gun and shot and missed as I returned fire, missing in turn.

Mohammed shrieked and fired as I dropped to the floor.

Elaine pumped two shots each into Jack and Mohammed.

"Sexist pigs!" she screamed as they fell.

Cigarette dangling from the corner of his lip, Abelard raised his pistol and shot her. As she slumped across the table top he mumbled "Father forgive me," rolling his eyes heavenward.

Lenora Hart and Suzy snatched their guns and fired simultaneously. Suzy caught the attorney dead center with a well-placed shot. Lenora's round caught the shoulder of Suzy's blouse, tearing through fabric but missing flesh.

"Your cut's a moot point now, Lenora *darling,*" said Suzy as Lenora Hart crumpled to her knees, gurgling up bloody bubbles as she died.

She turned her gun on the priest. There was a sharp *tak! tak!,* and Abelard jerked forward, then back, striking his head against the kitchen counter as he hit the floor, dead.

I rose on one knee. The length of the room between us, Suzy Anger coolly aimed her gun at my head. "Tell me where the money is, Johnny." The pistol barrel stared at me like a black, ugly little eye.

"We can share it, like I said before," she said. "Go away. Just the two of us."

"No dice," I said, standing and fighting the pain in my leg. "I don't want to end up like Von Schulte, or God knows how many others before him."

The knife wound began to throb. I resisted a black wave of unconsciousness that crested, then subsided in my head.

"I'm going to get my friend," I said. "I'm taking us out of here."

She tightened her grip on the trigger. "I'm afraid I can't let you do that, Johnny."

A third huge wave crashed against the home, tilting it violently. Grabbing the edge of the counter to regain her equilibrium, Suzy Anger aimed and fired. The hammer clicked on an empty chamber.

Cursing, she threw the pistol at me and lunged for Jack's loose thirty-eight sliding across the floor, losing it among the pile of corpses. The house was now at a sharp angle, teetering at the cliff's edge. The plywood flooring, torn from its cement slab foundation, began to buckle.

She groped for the pistol and found it.

I was sliding feet-first toward her as she aimed and fired, exactly when the lights flickered, then died.

A sliver of flame split the darkness. A bullet whizzed past me, striking a chair and knocking it backward.

I returned fire, and heard the thump of the bullet as it hit flesh.

There was a groan in the darkness.

"Johnny. Help me, please. I'm shot."

It was a sorrowful whimper, like a new puppy left alone and motherless in a cardboard box in the night.

I moved toward the sound of her voice, cautiously feeling my way across the floor, crawling over dead bodies. She may have been wounded, but she was still dangerous. My pistol at the ready, I found her sitting with her back pressed against the kitchen counter, clutching her stomach with both hands. Jack's gun lay useless at her side.

She smiled. "We could have gone away together, Johnny."

"I never believed you about that," I said. "I never believed you about anything."

"Then why did you come for me? I thought you were in love with me."

"Hardly. I wanted to find out what happened to my friend, that's all."

"Nothing more?" There was genuine pain in her voice, and not from my bullet lodged in her gut.

"Nothing," I lied.

She gazed at her stomach, looked up at me and managed a weak grin. "It hurts," she said, clutching at her wound. Blood leaked from between her fingers and streaked red the puddles of black water on the floor.

I extended my hand.

"Grab hold," I said.

She reached out. The tips of our fingers touched like cautious antennae groping in the dark.

She coughed, wincing in pain. "Everything went wrong, from start to finish. Johnny . . ."

She never finished the sentence. With a somber sigh, the house slowly slid down the muddy cliff, settling onto the beach ten feet below.

There was a shudder, and then the rending cadence of two by fours tearing away from the foundation as the waves ripped out the back of the house, hungrily sucking at its contents. The floor curled, but held. I felt her hand slip away from mine as she slid into the jaws of the storm.

"Johhhny!" she screamed as she was swept away into the icy waters.

I heard a long, mournful shriek and realized it was me bellowing as the lake sucked her under. I threw the pistol down and hammered the floor with my fist. She had made a fool of me, had tried to kill me, yet I felt a stabbing pain, a profound emptiness, in my heart. Go figure.

Frigid water lapping at my knees quickly brought me back to the seriousness of my situation.

The lake had eaten away the back of the home, and now the rapacious waves began to smash it from the inside.

I crab-walked on toes and fingertips out of the kitchen and found the bedroom where Virgil lay tied by the wrists to the bedposts. Clad only in his outlandish heart-studded boxer shorts, blood flowed from his mouth. His feet were peppered with grotesque burn marks from Mohammed's and Hakeem's cigarettes. There was a puckered bullet wound in his shoulder, where he'd first been shot. His jaw swelled obscenely from Fat's makeshift dental work.

"You look like hell, Virgil," I said.

He saw me and smiled that idiot smile of his, and I had a hard time believing all that I had heard about him could ever be true.

"Johnny," he lisped. "I knew you'd come for me. You wouldn't let a friend down."

"That's right, partner," I said as I fiddled with his bonds.

"Johnny, you know where the money is, don't you?"

"I do."

"I knew you'd figure it out. You're smart."

I untied one hand. He grasped my arm and squeezed.

"You take that money, Johnny. And that girl of yours and the two of you get the hell out of here. Find sunshine and beaches. Make babies. Drink rum."

"Sure, Virgil, sure. You just hold steady, partner, and we'll be out of here in a few seconds."

The house suddenly titled. I could feel it floating away, like a rudderless ship, into the merciless waves.

His grip became desperate, like a pipe wrench clamped onto my arm. "You have to go Johnny."

"Don't you see, Virgil?" I said, working at his knots with my free hand. "If I leave you here, and you die, all of this--everything we've suffered through in the last twenty-four hours--the torture, the deaths, the lies, the deceit--will have been for nada, amigo."

His voice grew weaker, became a pitiful squeak. "Oh, no, Johnny. It's the end of a terrible twenty years for me. I can come clean now, and know that at least some good will come from what I done to my friends, and their families."

His lip quivered, and I thought he was going to cry. "You listen to me!" he said. "You take that girl and make the most of what I'm giving you! Don't let me die for nothing!"

"You're not going to die. We're getting you out of here. Everything will be back to the way it was, you'll see."

"Uh, uh," he said. "I'm through. You go now."

He closed his eyes and died. It was that simple. He was here one second, the next he was gone.

I cursed and screamed and fumbled at the knot securing his other arm to the bedpost.

How long I stayed at his bedside and worked at those knots I don't know, but the water was at the top of his mattress (and up to my waist--me shivering with the cold) when I finally was forced to leave. I waded out of the home and clawed my way up the muddy face of the cliff. The blowing snow clawed at my face, burning my cheeks. I stood at the edge of the precipice watching the home slowly drift seaward as it collapsed into itself, sucked into the lake by the inexorable pounding of the surf.

As the waves smashed the house, I limped to my cab and opened the trunk. I dragged Von Schulte's body to the edge of the cliff and tossed it over. A giant wave like a curly-headed Tsunami in an ancient Japanese print; only this one muddy brown with a churning frothy white edge, broke out of the storm, slammed the shoreline, snatched Von Schulte's body and fled with it seaward. The corpse surfaced, rolling on the crest of the wave, then sank out of sight.

I rolled the carpet and put it back into the trunk. I'd burn it in the morning. The snow would cover my tracks. As a kid, the lake had been my playground, and I knew it well. In cold waters like these, bodies many times sank, never to rise. They would be picked clean by crayfish and lawyers (the fish, not the courtroom thugs) and their bones would settle deep into the silt at depths nearing one thousand feet. Or they could be swept along on a long, inexorable journey into Huron, Superior, Erie or Ontario and the bodies would wash up on some foreign shore, if they ever surfaced at all. If they did surface, it would take a million Sherlock Holmes to piece together the puzzle. The only intact clue was the yellow Dodge. Stolen, with fake plates and meticulously wiped of prints.

When all I could see were scattered shards of flotsam and jetsam bobbing on the waves I intoned an abbreviated Kaddish for Virgil and Suzy Anger and turned my back on the lake.

I climbed into the cab and drove myself to a hospital.

***

The doctor who stitched me up was an old friend. I had painted a family portrait for him a few years back, gratis.

"Just take care of me when the time comes," I'd said as I handed him his painting. "In lieu of insurance."

The time had come. He injected my wound with a series of Novocain shots that hurt like hell. I told him so.

"Better to take a little pain now, than a big pain later on," he said. I didn't like the tone of his voice. He sounded like he was having a good time. I told him that, too.

"I don't know what happened," he said as he skillfully snipped the last stitch. "But it's obvious that somebody stuck you with a knife. I should call the police."

"But you won't," I replied.

"I could get in trouble for this; if you were into something dirty."

"You know me better than that."

"I don't know you at all, Johnny Jump. Nobody does."

He called a nurse in to administer a tetanus shot.

"Hey," he said, snapping his fingers. "Have you heard Picasso died?"

I lay stunned, blindsided by the revelation.

"Did you hear me?" he said. "Picasso died?"

"What?" I said in genuine shock. My man Pablo, gone?

"I'll get you the paper. You can read it for yourself."

It couldn't be true. Pablo was a man for the ages, immortal. Not now, I begged. Not today. No more pain. No more horror.

A stocky nurse in a starched white uniform entered the room. "Turn over, hon," she said, preparing my injection in a businesslike manner.

I obeyed mechanically, flopped onto my stomach as the she pushed the needle into my quarter-black-ass. She daubed the hole with alcohol and taped a gauze patch over the wound.

"Since when does a tetanus shot get delivered in the fanny?" I asked her.

"Since I decided I wanted a look-see at that tight ass of yours," she said.

I wasn't up for her good-natured flirting. My God, didn't she know Pablo was dead? "That's taking unfair advantage," I said.

"It is." She kissed her fingers and gave my rump a gentle pat.

The doctor returned with the paper and handed it to me.

"Here," he said. "In black and white. Five column headline above the fold."

I slowly mouthed the words as I lay on my stomach on the emergency room bed, trembling with emotion as I read the story.

Widow grieves, world mourns Picasso's death

MOUGINS, France (UPI)— Pablo Picasso's widow has not left the artist's body since he died and is still overcome with grief, the gardener for the household said today.

The Spanish painter, who has been called the most influential creator of modern day art died at 11:40 a.m. (5:40 a.m. EST) Sunday of heart failure following congestion of the lungs. He was 91.

A man many called the Michelangelo of the 20th Century and a tireless worker who created 200,000 works of art in three quarters of a century, Picasso lived the last 10 years of his life as a recluse. Even the mayor of nearby Vallouris was turned away from the iron gate barring the little road to his tile-roofed, vine-covered stone villa. . .

. . . Admirers and artists around the world poured out tributes.

Some critics question the greatness of some aspects of Picasso's work . . .

I slapped the paper against the emergency room table in disgust. "Some critics questioned the greatness of some aspects of Picasso's work?" Idiots! How could they even begin to attempt to judge the man or his work?

I continued reading.

. . . but most agreed his brilliance lay in the unmatched variety of his output—from abstract to realistic painting, from paper collages to ceramics.

There were reports on the French Riviera two weeks ago that Picasso suffered a heart attack in this sun-washed land where the Spanish-born artist had lived in protest against the regime of Francisco Franco. But still his gardener, Jaques Barra, 55, said the death was a shock.

"At noon Sunday, I was in the garden and Madame Picasso came out, very upset, and said "My husband just died."

Picasso died as he lived—working feverishly . . .

. . . Friends said he recently worked on three or four paintings at once. He was seen in the villages of the Riviera only occasionally, usually to visit his Cannes tailor who made him velvet trousers and bright checked suits.

"I don't like to go out because I prefer to work," he said recently. "I also need love. I have spent my life loving and I love everything passionately."

All the death and destruction I'd seen the day before, and now this, the biggest shock. I had envisioned Pablo as superhuman, an icon who would live forever. Not so.

I quietly folded the paper, slipped out of my hospital gown and into my damp clothes.

Wet, miserable, in pain; I limped like a zombie through the emergency room corridors. I passed the doctor in the hall.

"You mind if I keep this?" I asked him, flashing the folded newspaper.

"Be my guest," he said. "I remembered that Picasso was one of your heroes, wasn't he?"

I shrugged. I have had only three heroes in my life: Grandma Jones, my Polish Jew grandfather and Pablo Picasso; and now the last of them was dead.

I thanked the doc for the newspaper and exited the hospital.

I stood outside the glass doors and buried my head in my hands. It was the third time in my life I had cried. The first was at Grandma Jones' funeral, the second was at Virgil's storm-tossed bedside.

My man Pablo.

Dead.

PART SEVEN
APRIL 9, 1973

Jennifer handed me my Seven and Seven. "Here you go, Johnny."

I returned from the hospital and found her waiting on my doorstep. Sparky had phoned her in an effort to find out where the hell I (and his cab) had gone to. She had gently bathed me and then tucked me into bed and I had slept through the night and into the afternoon.

When I woke, I found her preparing a dinner of roast beef, green beans and mashed potatoes (my favorite); the scent of which brought back memories of Grandma Jones, bent over her old emerald green and white enameled Chambers gas stove while I stood at her knee, taking in the wonderful aroma of her down-home cooking, listening intently to her earthy patter.

"I called Sparky and he sent somebody to pick the cab up," Jennifer said. "He was only a little bit mad, when I told him you'd been hurt. He told me to tell you to take the week off. Your job will be waiting for you when you come back."

"Thanks." I slid behind her and wrapped my arms around her waist, nibbled at her neck. Jennifer is tall, five-ten, with cascading dishwater blonde hair and a strong face anchored by a noble Roman nose. She has strong legs and heavy breasts and large, muscular hands. But it all jibes and she is considered to be a very attractive woman.

What is most appealing about Jennifer though, is the soft, yielding center at the very core of her being. Not weak, or mushy; but a spirit that can take anything life can dish out, absorb it like a sponge and make the best of it.

I sipped at the highball and felt the whiskey rush through my veins like a warm electric fire. I stirred a finger in the drink, ice cubes tinkling against the glass. Jennifer snuggled next to me on the couch and slipped under my arm, her head on my shoulder.

"Mmm, this is nice," she said.

It was. Especially after the previous day's antics. Suzy Anger had been fire and ice. Jennifer was a comforting, powerful, steady warmth. I felt I could crawl inside her and sleep there forever. Hell, maybe I just would do that.

We sat sipping our drinks, staring at the wall for a few long minutes before I broke the silence.

"Virgil is dead," I said.

She stiffened, shock chiseling deep furrows in her face. "What?"

"He was an old man," I lied. "He lived past his time."

"Where did he die? How did he die?"

"Trust me on this, Jennifer. He went out in style. In a few days I'll tell you everything."

She cried softly. "I loved that old man," she said.

"I did, too." But I was thinking about Pablo.

She settled back under my arm, but I could see the spell was broken. She was too shaken by the news of Virgil's death.

"I'm going to check the roast," she said, taking her drink with her in the kitchen. I heard her opening the oven door, lift the cover off the roasting pan, then close the oven door. She was talking to herself.

"What the . . . ?" she mumbled. Then louder, "Johnny, what's this?"

She walked back into the living room and shoved her drink under my nose. Glinting in the bottom of her glass was a bright metal safety deposit box key. She had cooled her drink with the ice cube that Virgil had hidden the key inside. He must have known Suzy Anger and her friends were hot on his trail and secreted the key in the ice tray, knowing full well I never used ice cubes, preferring cold beer over mixed drinks. The ice cube tray always sat encrusted with frost, forgotten in my unused freezer.

"Damned if I know," I responded. But I did know. Virgil had a small bundle of cash, money scrounged from friends and strangers. The key would fit a box to the bank where he kept that cash. I was sure of that.

Was there a million dollars cash in that box? I could take the key and open it and find out. Virgil had said for me to pocket the money and spirit Jennifer away to where there were bright sand beaches and endless sunshine.

Then I thought of Pablo, laboring in his early years, broke but full of desire and ambition. I always thought he had created his greatest works before the art world discovered and then worshipped him, throwing money at him.

Would he have had the fire in his belly if he had been born into great wealth?

I doubted it. Money was always trouble, never worth the effort it took to accumulate it. Money destroyed lives.

The key glinted in her glass, beckoning me. I fished it out and held it between finger and thumb.

"What if I told you that this was the key to a safety-deposit box and that in that box was one million dollars?"

She looked at me, slightly cock-eyed. "You're joking."

"I'm not."

She pursed her lips sternly. "Johnny, don't play games with me. It's not right."

"It's not a game, Jennifer, and I've never been more serious in my life. There's a catch, though. It's not clean money. People have died because of it. A lot of people."

"You're serious?"

"Yes. The money's there and it's ours if we want it. It was the reason Virgil died. He left this key here because he wanted me--us--to have the money. The last words he said to me were "take that girl of yours to someplace with bright beaches. Drink rum. Make babies."

"One million dollars." Her voice had a plaintive, far-away tone, like a kid before Christmas, dreaming of gifts to come.

"It's your call," I said.

"If he died for the money, Johnny, and he wanted you to have it; then I think you should have it."

She'd resolved my dilemma. We bundled up and slogged through the snow-bound streets, past merchants cursing as they shoveled sidewalks, trying to salvage what was left of the Easter shopping season. The bank was six blocks away, on the far end of downtown. We handed the key to the security guard manning the vault.

"Right this way sir," he said. We followed him into the vault and down a short hall.

"Your box is here," he said, gesturing to a small slot with a keyhole. He unlocked it and slid out a box with another keyhole.

"You may open it in privacy in that room over there," he said, pointing to a narrow door.

My heart sank. A million dollars couldn't fit into a box this small. Maybe the entire thing had been a hoax from the very start.

The guard led us into the room. "Call me when you're finished," he said, closing the door behind him.

Hand shaking, I slid the key into the keyhole and opened the box. Inside I found a note and a bank book. I opened the note first.

"What does it say?" asked Jennifer, leaning over my shoulder.

I read it aloud for her benefit.

Dear Johnny,

If you're reading this, then I'm probably dead and you've probably found out all about me.

I told you I done bad things in my life. I been on the run for twenty years, and in all that time nobody showed me one bit of kindness, until I met you. You took me in without knowing one thing about me. You fed me, give me a warm place to stay and pin money for beer.

You been good to me, Johnny, and I want to repay the favor. Remember those papers I asked you to sign for me as a witness last year? I said they was for relatives back home? You didn't even look at what you was signing, just scribbled your name down like I asked. I opened a bank account in your name in Miami, using those papers. They got your signature, and your picture, too.

I want you to fly to Florida, get the money and take Jennifer to British Honduras. They call it Belize now. They got beautiful beaches, great rum and they speak English, too!

I bled for that money, Johnny. Every penny of it. It's rightfully mine and I give it to you.

Your Pal,
Virgil

I set the letter down and opened the bank book. It was there, stamped and verified, just as Virgil had said. One million dollars, deposited in the name of Johnny Jump.

"Oh, Johnny," Jennifer whispered. The pleasure in her voice was for my good fortune, not hers.

"Would you like to leave this town, maybe travel to the tropics and live there for a while?" I asked.

"Johnny. If you're really leaving, I'll definitely go with you."

She held clenched fists on her lap, as if she were a boxer psyching up in her corner.

"It'll get me out of the life, Johnny. I figured I had at least five more years of dancing left before I'd have enough salted away to quit. I swear, if I had to fight one more puking drunk trying to fondle my tits, I was going to get a gun and blow his brains out."

"You don't have to do this if you don't want to," she added. "You don't owe me anything."

"No strings attached, Jennifer. I wouldn't ask if I didn't want you with me."

I pocketed the note and the bank book and kissed her on the cheek. "Let's get back home."

Back in my apartment, I mixed us fresh drinks. I'd phone the travel agency later and book a flight to Miami. Then I'd eat supper with Jennifer, phone Sparky and tell him I was through.

I stared at my unfinished portrait of Virgil. I'd leave it with Ned, have it shipped to me when the paint dried.

I'd finish that portrait on the sand beaches of Belize, under the bright tropical sun. A magnum opus; a paean to the gentle old man with the haunted past. Adieu, Virgil. Adios, mi amigo.

I would paint fantasies of Jennifer on those beaches. Tanned and sleek. Naked, Sand clinging to her hollows and curves, tiny waves licking at her toes. Like Paul Gauguin in paradise, rendering his dream-induced canvases of dusky, raven-haired women. Noa Noa.

We would snorkel in crystal clear lagoons, indulge in spicy tropical eats and quaff fiery drinks concocted of exotic fruit juices and thick black rum.

At night we would dance to the sounds of guitars and steel drums.

Later, we would make love in the moonlight as tropical birds trilled in the palm trees.

I would not dwell on Suzy Anger. She was dead, and her story with her.

All who had been involved but me were now memories, buried at sea.

That night, with Jennifer snug in my arms, I dreamed of Suzy Anger's beautiful corpse, picked clean--luminous skeleton waltzing with drowned mariners and sea creatures in the icy black depths--a cotillion of fishes and bones.

Requiescat in pace

I would leave them--as old bones should be--at peace.

PART EIGHT-
INTERMEZZO

Picasso's body entombed in crypt

MOUGINS, France (UPI)— The body of Pablo Picasso was removed today from his hilltop villa before dawn and entombed without ceremony in a crypt at his chateau 60 miles away.

The body was placed in the chapel of the chateau, a home Picasso bought at Aix en Provence in 1958.

A spokesman for the undertaker said only Picasso's 46 year old widow Jacqueline, his son Paolo and a niece from Spain, Mrs. Dolores Vilato-Ruiz, were present when the body was placed in the crypt.

"There was no funeral ceremony," the spokesman said. "He is in the crypt of his chateau. The family received permission yesterday to take the body there."

Picasso, a giant of 20th century art, died at his Moulins villa Sunday of heart failure following lung congestion. He was 91.

He had lived in seclusion at the Mougins home for 10 years and remained alone, except for his immediate family.

A nephew of Picasso, the Spanish painter Xavias Villato, arrived with his wife in a taxi at the gates of the Moulin villa. They appeared astonished when told the family had left with the body.

Art lovers the world over worshipped Picasso but only a handful showed up at Mougins to pay their respects. Those who did were barred from entering the house by Picasso's widow.

The loudspeakers announced the boarding call for our plane. I abandoned the newspaper to my chair, stood and stretched. As I followed Jennifer to the boarding ramp, I gazed out the bank of windows, across the O'Hare tarmac and into the wide blue sky.

I heard Virgil's whisper, like the sound of the sea in a shell. "Don't let me die for nothing, Johnny," he had said. With his dying words, he had pointed the way.

I felt a rush of fulfillment, and smiled.

I dropped my bags and pounded my chest and howled.

"Yes!" I cried. People gawked as if I had escaped from a loony bin.

I raised my clenched fists high, clutching at the firmament. It all made sense to me now. Virgil would not have died in vain. He would live on in my work.

I eyeballed the multitudes, all who had stopped to stare. The hell with them! I was suddenly filled with a great truth; in the power of my song, in the strength of my brushes and canvas and paint, that they would never--could never--comprehend.

I had a vision of ancient Pablo, afloat on his death bed in that faraway villa, breathing his last; surrounded by the ghosts of his many mistresses, visions of unfinished canvases.

"Don't you see it?" I shouted. "Look!"

A thousand heads craned upward. There was a collective sigh as a muscular cloud eclipsed the sun. From behind it, golden fingers crowned the darkened sky.

People began to applaud, to whistle.

I cheered them. They saw. They knew.

That cloud was Pablo's spirit, sketching shadows on the heavens.

The End

Made in the USA
Lexington, KY
28 January 2014